Commuting.

An Underground World

Written by Stephen Down
(Who's he?)

Disclaimer announcement

Any tips or advice found within are very unlikely to have any effect on your commuter situation. This book and the accompanying illustrations are sold with the understanding that neither the author nor his fellow commuters have any real idea what they are talking about. TfL certainly don't endorse it. Your guess is as good as ours.

With thanks

Muchas gracias to my wife for her support and ruthless honesty, both in life and throughout this book's journey.

To my Sister and Nisha for helping with the edits, and Paul for the amazing illustrations. Also, to Laura, Nat and Helen for the marketing assistance.

To TfL for transporting me around London.

And finally, to all you lovely commuters for making this book possible.

The Approach

The Oxford English Dictionary defines the term 'Commute' as:

"To travel some distance between one's home and place of work on a regular basis."

An alternative definition of the term 'Commute' is:

"To travel **miserably with millions of other people**, some distance between one's home and place of work on a regular basis. **All in disruptive conditions, enduring too much close contact with other terribly annoying human beings, for a considerable amount of money.**"

Let's Get Moving

The majority of us do it. The majority of us hate it. Whether you travel to work three, four or even five days a week, commuting is something that we all get frustrated by. You're one of the lucky ones if you actually enjoy your travel into work.

We all have different ways of commuting:

- car
- bike
- taxi/Uber (every day? Alright flashy pants)
- bus
- train
- tube
- walking (yes, apparently people still participate in this ancient past time)
- snowboarding (obviously weather permitting. My sister was lucky enough to board to work when she lived in France)

Most of us commuters travel at the same time of day, resulting in what is more commonly referred to as the 'morning and evening rush'. This causes substantial congestion on roads and public transport systems. In a world where populations are forever expanding, surely the tribulations of commuting will only worsen?

Apparently, the average worker spends nearly 200 hours a year commuting to and from work[1]. Take a minute and consider what you could do with an extra 200 hours:

- Get healthy and go to the gym (nah!)
- Spend more time with friends and family (that'd be nice!)
- Study for a degree or learn a new skill (use my brain? Sounds exhausting!)

Or, more likely, laze around in your PJs on the sofa, eating junk food and catching up on the latest trash TV shows. Yep, that'd be me.

During my time spent commuting on the London Underground, I have noticed a whole different world with unspoken rules (for example: the silence, the averted eyes, the blank stares, and the ever-important A to B mentality). This book will (hopefully) let you sit back and enjoy some unforgettable and often comical real-life events, compiled from my individual experiences on public transport in London.

---

[1] Sourced from http://www.thisismoney.co.uk/money/news/article-2061409/The-average-worker-spends-weeks-year-commuting-statistics-reveal.html?ito=feeds-newsxml)

The Commuter Rules

Rule 1: ~~Look miserable at all times~~ Sit/stand/crouch in silence. Whatever you do, **DO NOT TALK**; this will cause excessive staring and rather stern, annoyed looks.

Rule 2: When on escalators, slow people (mostly tourists) who are not in a rush, must stick to the right-hand lane (designated slow lane). The left-hand lane is to be used for overtaking (similar to a French motorway), for those who wish to walk/run/sprint or trip up.

Rule 3: When a train arrives on the platform, please wait for fellow commuters to evacuate the train *first* before bundling on. Standing in the middle of the doors when people are trying to get off = unwise.

Rule 4: Give up your seat if you see one of the following category of persons: pregnant ladies, disabled individuals, people of the elderly variety or those that are severely hungover.

Rule 5: Remember to bring some form of entertainment to pass time. Main examples include: phones, music, books, newspapers or magazines. For the more advanced, long-term commuter, just go to sleep. Failure to adhere to this rule will lead to excessive boredom.

Rule 6: Be prepared to get *extremely* close to fellow human beings that you do not know and are unlikely to ever meet again. This may include (depending on your height or stature) being under people's armpits or having to sit on people.

Rule 7: Try to keep your centre of gravity. True commuters can spot tourists/rookie travellers on mere balance alone. Wobbly legs are a clear indication of a lack of experience, which – even to the untrained eye – exposes your commuting vulnerability. In most cases, this can lead to extreme cases of embarrassment, potential seat loss and a high chance of losing any remaining 'street cred' with the kids.

Rule 8: Breathe in. When in a rush (which is at all times), find gaps wherever you are going. It doesn't matter how small - you *can* get through it.

Rule 9: Do not fart on a crowded train or, if you have no other option, make sure that you are close to someone who can be easily blamed.

Rule 10: Know every route off by heart when it comes to tube lines and getting around London. This is a sure-fire way to impress any out-of-towners. Don't worry, you can always make it up, they won't be any wiser.

Book Map

Stop 1: Awkward Situations

\<Baby on Board\>

Uh oh. Awkward situation on the tube. Such events as these are mostly entertaining to witness but are terrifyingly, horrifically, painfully compromising to be involved in. Thankfully, I only viewed this awkward affair from the front row (leant against that transparent pane next to the seats).

A commuter rule that really grates on me if broken is the all-singing, all-dancing, giving up your seat to a pregnant lady. It's just plain rude. There have been numerous occasions where I have seen people look up and notice that a pregnant lady is standing but then quickly drop their heads and hope that no-one has noticed. All so they can keep their seat and use the excuse of "I was blissfully unaware, I had no idea she was pregnant." Whatever. We all saw you. In my eyes, it's the King of Tube-Rudeness.

So, picture this. A man was sitting down reading the paper, when the train stopped and a crowd of people got off, to be replaced by a fresh batch of commuters. He looked up and spotted a lady. This is where the confusion began. I was sure he knew the rule and would quite happily adhere to it. He seemed like a polite person who would always be willing to surrender his precious seat for a pregnant lady. However, the problem was:

·   She wasn't wearing the TfL 'Baby on board' badge (Incidentally, I *love* the person who invented this).
·   She had a stomach with a bump.
·   This stomach with a bump *may* have just been her carrying a little bit of extra weight.

In my head, the situation was going to go one of three ways.

1)   He would offer his seat and she would thank him kindly, adding "Standing for two isn't fun." Phew. Potential crisis averted.

2)   Shy, unsure and incredibly indecisive, he would begin to weigh up the pregnancy conundrum and decide not to offer his seat. Place the ball in her court. If she was pregnant, she could always come and ask, right?

3)   In true British-style he'd be polite and offer his seat. She would reply with a frantic, confused look, considering why a random stranger would offer this. Seeing him glance at her stomach she'd connect the dots. While this was happening, he would already be at the halfway point between sitting and standing, unsure of what was going to happen

next, eagerly awaiting her response. She'd turn bright red; his face would flush and then silence (apart from the little 'hush' of the crowd as they would await the main event). She'd respond with, "Thanks, but I'm okay," meaning she wasn't pregnant and he had more than likely deeply offended her. She'd need more Kleenex while watching the next episode of One Born Every Minute.

Of course, you guessed it- he chose option number three. We've all been there haven't we?

The poor man sat down, obviously deeply self-conscious. From the look in his eyes I could tell he was wishing the tube seat would swallow him up.

'The awkward tube situation of the year' award goes to...

THAT MAN!

Time for him to come on up and collect the highly acclaimed and sought-after trophy, from the not-so-pregnant lady that he had just offended.

Here's my plea – respect to pregnant women. Having to go to work is hard enough, let alone having to tube it with another human being inside you. Can you think of anything worse than having to deal with a commute like that every day while feeling nauseous and hungry, needing the toilet and having sore limbs from carrying around extra weight? Well, maybe not noticing that your zip has been undone this whole time and you're wearing the only remaining clean pair of boxers... which are a luminous yellow. Whoops – better get the washing on.

\<Babybels\>

I grabbed a seat at Waterloo with no-one around me. Embankment comes along and two guys sit either side of me. Nothing funny yet. Wait for it. I'm getting to it.

To say these guys weren't your average size would be an even bigger understatement than the size of their bulging guts. As their gigantic weight pummelled the already worn and tired fabric seats, my feet lifted off the ground. It wasn't just my arms that were squashed, no, all my internal organs were merging into one. My eyes, nose, cheeks and mouth suddenly compressed, resulting in an extreme pout that even Victoria Beckham would be proud of. Breathing was hard, or anything that required some level of concentration.

The guys were shaped like Babybels and their rolls of flab popped out between the arm rests. They didn't smell particularly great either. So, I scrunched my nose up, closed my eyes and prayed.

Please get off at the next stop, please get off at the next stop, please get off at the next stop.

They didn't. Or the next one. Or the one after that. I began to understand the perils of chafing in stuffy conditions.

I needed to get off, but realised I couldn't move. My arms, legs and torso were completely trapped. Embedded in-between their massive, unnecessary masses. Frightened beyond belief, I was forced to ignore all British politeness and address my big fat predicament.

"Would you mind getting up as I'm kind of stuck in-between you both?"

I tried to be as discreet and polite about it as you possibly could under the circumstances. From the looks on their faces, they weren't impressed (did they really think I wanted to ask them such a question?). My fellow commuters showered the whole carriage with discomfort. Like fat from an over-used fryer, the tension was literally dripping off the walls.

In the end, one of the guys stood up so I could just about launch myself off the tube before the doors closed. It took two days to remove the pout from my face. I think it will be a while before I choose to digest a Babybel again.

11

Stop 2: Travelling with Little People

\<Smelly Oysters\>

The morning bus journey provided some great entertainment in the form of one little kid. I'd say he was around the age of six. I honestly love kids, they can provide you with some top-notch comedy moments, mainly due to naivety or honesty.

Karl: Mum, can I ask you a question?
Mum: Yes, I suppose so.
Karl: Why does it smell bad?
Mum: Because you just farted.
Karl: Oh, yeah.
Karl: Mum?
Mum: Yes.
Karl: Why do farts smell?
Mum: Cause you don't eat enough greens. (Clever work by mum there.)

Karl: Really? But I don't like greens. Hmm, I'm happy having smelly farts if it means I no longer have to eat greens.

Mum: You might be, but the rest of the people on this bus probably aren't.

PAUSE

Karl: Mum?
Mum: Yes.
Karl: What's that smell?
Mum: You again.

PAUSE

Karl: Okay, I'll eat more greens.

There's an important life lesson for all the youngsters out there. We're rooting for you.

\<Commuter entertainment\>

It's 'back to school' day, and whilst this means that buses are far busier, at least it makes for another entertaining journey with kids.

The first sproglet seemed to enjoy one of the bus stop names: 'Lewis Gardens'. She liked it so much that she started singing about it.

"Lewis Gardens, Lewis Gardens, the bus is going to stop at Lewis Gardens."

What completely made this song, and why I blame myself for not filming it on my phone, was some seven-year-old boy then proceeded to beat-box over the top of her. Brilliant. Both mums were trying, without success, to get them to "Shut up!" in their own words.

When these kids left to go to school, thankfully they were replaced by a young girl who seemed to enjoy pointing at everything and saying what it was. Here are some examples:

1) "Seat!"
2) "Window!"
3) "Seat next to window!"
4) "Woman!"
5) "Tree!"
6) "Sad man!"
7) "Bell!"
8) "Man with big nose!"
9) "Sweaty man!"
10) "Unicorn!"

That certainly put a smile on all commuter faces.

\<Being Taught a Lesson\>

Half term arrived, and a scruffy eight-year-old boy called... ermmm.... Ron (definitely made up and probably something to do with my recent viewing of a certain Will Ferrell film) was with his dad on the platform, when he noticed a poster for Black Panther.

Ron: Dad, are we going to watch that soon?

Dad: Your Mum and I will be, you're not. It's a 12A.

Ron: Yeah, but that means you can take me if you are over twelve. You are over twelve right Dad?

(*Ron - sarcasm is the lowest form of wit don't you know*).

Dad: Yes, I am much older than twelve.

Ron: We can go tomorrow then?

Dad: Ask your mother.

Ron: Now?

Dad: No, not now, later.

Ron: But I might forget later.

Dad: Here's hoping.

Ron: Can we go tonight?

Dad: What did I say?

Ron: Pass me your phone and I'll call her.

Dad: I'm using it.

Ron: Playing Angry Birds again I bet.

Dad: I'm answering e-mails.

Ron: I want to play on it.

Dad: I thought you wanted to call your mum.

Ron: Oh yeah, can I do that?

Dad: Depends how well behaved you are at work today.

Ron: I promise.

Dad: Prove it, if you're well behaved all day, I'll let you call her.

Ron: Until 3pm?

Dad: I work until 6pm son, not 3pm.

Ron: But school...

Dad: Is not the same as work.

Ron: How about until lunchtime?

Dad: You're not the greatest negotiator. Starts... now!

Ron: Okay Dad, I will show you ultimate politeness.

Tube pulled into the station, Ron stood to the side to let someone off. There were plenty of available seats and so after offering them around, they both sat down. When the train pulled into Highgate, more passengers came on and Ron immediately jumped to attention and offered his seat to the first person to come near him, with a nonchalant "I have the youngest legs here, I can stand."

He then announced to the whole carriage that if anyone needed any help with anything, to just ask.

At Archway a lady got on with two suitcases and Ron offered to help, until he realised that the suitcases weighed more than him and he couldn't even lift the handles, let alone the contents. Another lady tried to take her coat off and he offered to hold her bag while she did so.

When we pulled into Camden, a pregnant lady got on, to the announcement of Ron:

"Pregnant woman aboard everybody, be careful, she has a mini human inside of her!"

As we left Euston, Ron perked up again:

Ron: Anyone want a sip of my Ribena?

Dad: Stop offering your lunch around the carriage.

Ron: I'm only being polite Dad.

Dad: What will you have left at lunch?

Ron: I'm sure I'll survive. Cheese sandwich anyone? Skips? Apple?

Dad: Alright, alright, I'll take you to see Black Panther tonight, just stop offering your lunch around.

Ron: SCORE. WHOOP WHOOP.

The modern-day child and manipulation at its best. Nice one Ron.

Tube Announcement:

"Sorry for the delay to your reading, the author has dropped his pen. Service will resume shortly when he finds it or buys a new one."

Stop 3: (Lack of) Awareness

The trait of being completely unaware of your surroundings is probably the most common characteristic that you will experience whilst commuting. I find it *very* irritating.

<Swinging Arms>

Have you ever experienced Excessively Sweeping Arm Movement (ESAM)? Come on, you know what I'm talking about.

I was on one of those travelator-thingys (not quite the same as in Gladiators - what a show!), but I couldn't overtake the lady in front of me because her arm was swinging so vigorously that I was deeply afraid for my crotch (which was at the same height as her swinging arm). I imagine that it'd compare to someone hitting you in the nuts with quite a sturdy, thick piece of wood (no pun intended).

Lads, it's not worth thinking about.

Ladies, it's not funny. No, really, it isn't.

"OUCH!" is what I would have said, but more likely I would have been silenced by the powerful mix of pain and disbelief.

Going into shock, keeled over on the moving travelator, curled up in a foetal position holding my nuts, and slowly being dragged to the end.

Here's how it could look. I know – I'm quite the artist.

As this would ultimately cause more disruption to fellow commuters (not to mention the sheer humiliation), I took the safe option, stayed where I was and avoided the ESAM.

However, this did mean that I missed my tube by three seconds and had to wait six minutes for another. That's right, six minutes of my life!!! Can you believe the audacity of that? Shock. Horror. I spent my journey considering this and concluded that it would have taken me over six minutes to get past the pain and agony of being smacked in the gonads, so it was better to take the hit (not literally) and be slightly late home.

\<Every Second Counts\>

I reckon TfL should hold lessons on how to move through the barriers in an efficient manner, or just how to stop being such a *dunce*.

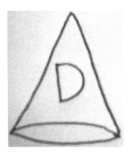

I've noticed recently, that in the evening rush hour, many individuals do some things that delay my journey by I'd say, about ten seconds. That may not be much to some people (or the majority), but for us hardened commuters, ten seconds is an eternity (10 seconds x 5 days x 52 weeks = 44 minutes wasted a year). Every second counts.

Does anyone else get annoyed when people race to the front of the ticket barrier, stop, and then proceed to spend what seems like two hours trying to find their Oyster card/contactless card/paper ticket? This is especially irritating when it's peak time and there are only three barriers to get through. This means 33.3333333333*% of the barriers are blocked. No Doubt the card is lodged in their bag, in between a banana, the Evening Standard and the kitchen sink.

All it needs is a split second of awareness before reaching the barrier to ensure that you are ready to swipe through. If your card isn't within easy reach, then why not take a step to one side and ensure you are out of the way of the never-ending flow of people? Huh? Why not?

Dunce.

Oh yeah, that would involve some self-awareness, which is an infrequent characteristic in this peculiar underground world.

Here's another one. Ever noticed the passengers who choose to hold their Oyster cards/contactless cards on the reader, and linger it there for longer than necessary? Enough so that they get through, but then I'm left with a 'Seek assistance' warning, a ten-second wait and about 4000 people behind me giving me the "You're an idiot and you've ruined my evening, I'm not going to be able to get home and do my ironing," look. Terrified, I attempt to respond with a "It wasn't me, it was the person in front's fault," but they all don't appear best pleased. I end up getting a response of "Whatever, stop making excuses you twat."

One final ticket barrier-related issue I need to vent about. Promise. Those people who stand pretty much on the barrier and swipe, and the system won't let them through. The individual stubbornly stands in that area for over twenty seconds, continuously swiping, oblivious to what they're doing wrong. Only when the guard shouts out loudly for the third, repetitive and now slightly irate time, "Stand back and then swipe!", does the individual listen. They finally step back, swipe and then totter on as if nothing was wrong, leaving the massive queue of commuters behind them without even the courtesy of a "Sorry," or a "Thanks," to the guard. Charming. I know what you're thinking. Don't speak.

<Queue-tastic>

Some stations on the London Underground are so busy that it is necessary for one of our favourite British traditions to be employed; queuing. Everyone loves to queue, right?

Stations such as London Bridge, Waterloo, Canary Wharf etc, become so busy at peak times that we must form an orderly queue. Otherwise, madness would ensue.

On many occasions, I've witnessed those who like to circumvent this rule and just barge straight in. It's normally after I've spent five minutes waiting for a train, where the queue is six people deep and it is pretty obvious to every person with any sense of awareness that we are all queuing for the next train. On what basis does someone think it is okay to jump the queue and walk on ahead of everyone else? Are they completely unaware of their surroundings or just plain rude?

Sometimes I let it go because I can't be bothered to cause a fuss (typical commuter response). Other times, I'm just too irritated and so end up rolling my eyes and making really insightful, sarcastic comments such as: "There is a queue you know," "Sorry, I didn't realise you are a more important human being than the rest of us, do go on ahead," or "Thanks for that. Love you." The last two normally get a good laugh from my fellow commuters.

\<Rule Breaks\>

Commuter Rule 1

I can imagine the looks on all your faces when you read about this rule break.

Gasp. Shock. Horror.

Let me explain the details. Two people were having a chat on the tube *while* sitting on different sides of the carriage – not even opposite each other! Such a blatant disregard for the official Commuter Rules (which obviously should be displayed at every London Underground station - I've made a note to inform TfL about this). Harsh stares were directed towards them from every direction. The young lady chatted away, fully aware of the disruption she was causing to fellow passengers. Did she care about the British disapproving looks that she was receiving? Not in the slightest.

It still amazes me to this day how loud two people talking to each other can sound on the tube, considering all the background noise from the motion of the train moving through the tunnel. For some reason, the train's rumbling doesn't disturb my reading (probably because I'm used to it, so I can tune it out). However, when someone starts talking, I cannot block out the sound of their voice from my head.

All I could hear was the story she was telling about teaching the children in her class about dinosaurs. Seemingly, one child was adamant that dinosaurs became extinct because

Santa flew down on his sleigh and threw a meteor at them (this was despite the laughter from his fellow classmates and stifled giggles from the teachers in the room). "It's true, it's true!" he proclaimed.

She went on to explain that this roaring statement came from the same student who had the previous week been called into the headteacher's office for covering the boys' toilets in wet toilet roll. Apparently, he flat out denied it, even though there was strong physical evidence linking him to the crime scene. He was covered from head to toe in bits of soggy toilet roll...

The young lady and her fellow rule breaker finally disembarked the train at Euston. I had to admit that her story allowed me to forgive the rule break as it made me giggle. However, the skeletal remains of dinosaurs probably didn't find it humerus.

Commuter Rule 2

I had three minutes to get from the top of Waterloo station down to the Northern line to catch the train to Mill Hill East. So, in true commuter style, I activated my excessively fast walking mode (probably the same speed as a light jog). Down the escalators I went; full speed.

BAM!

A lady on the right decided to purposively step out to the left, to the left, right in front of me and completely cut me up. I managed to stop myself in time before crashing into her, nearly losing my balance and falling head over heels down the escalator. Completely oblivious to the Commuter Rule that she had just broken, unaware that I even existed, she lazily continued to loiter in the left-hand lane (why?!? She was standing on the right, why then stand on the left, on the left, for no reason?).

Once at the bottom, she suddenly stopped. Surprise surprise (as Cilla used to say), I nearly fell into her again. It wasn't until this point that she emerged from blissful ignorance, now realising that I was standing behind her with quite the frantic look across my face. What made this even more frustrating was the fact that no-one else, absolutely no-one, had walked down the left-hand side apart from me, so she had managed to time her cutting-up-ness rather well. She must not have known about me, she must not have known about me.

Commuter Rule 3

Another rule break that really irritates me is the people wall block. The train pulls into the station and you make your way to the doors to disembark (or attempt to). What you are then faced with is a wall of people blocking your exit.

Stand-off time.

Are they going to realise the error of their ways and move to the side to allow you to get past, or will they just stand there looking like oblivious lemons?

I don't understand what is going through their heads as they stand on the platform, staring up at me, wondering why I'm not getting off the train. Surely any reasonable human being with any sense of logic would work out that if there is no way of getting off, then there is no way of getting on. Simples, right? Obviously not.

I've lost count of how many times this has happened. Maybe they expect me to crowd surf over the top of them? Thinking about it, maybe I will do that next time. It sounds way more fun than having to huff, puff and push my way through like a Warrington Wolves rugby player.

Stop 4: Busker's Got Talent

\<Frank H'obo\>

Thank god for home time. Nothing beats that fruitful Friday feeling whilst on the tube home, listening to the Boss and considering what that first drink will be at the pub - a pint of beer or, go all alternative, and start with a shot of Limoncello?

At the bus stop outside Archway I was unexpectedly given the pleasure of meeting a strong candidate for 'Busker's Got Talent'. I have named him 'Frank H'obo' (not his real name, obviously).

Frank H'obo was 6ft, with glasses and a fluffy, black, neglected and ungroomed moustache. He wore a beanie hat, long black coat, dark jeans and one of those JD t-shirts. He was carrying bags within bags, within bags. He also smelt (and not in a J'adore, by Christian Dior, way).

Frank H'obo decided that Friday evening, on the 43 to Friern Barnet, was the best time to bust out a rather splendid rendition of 'Another Brick in the wall' by Pink Floyd. Then he belted out the Sex Pistols, followed by a random (but not completely unexpected given the circumstances) rant about David Cameron being a dick (this was back when he was Prime Minister). He went silent for a minute and the other passengers held their breath (undoubtedly not in anticipation of hearing this talent sing, but because his odour was increasing, stimulated by his vigorous performance). Unfortunately, he then continued, treating us to his own version of Slade and 'Merry Xmas Everybody' (in October, so slightly early). This was followed by the Clash (better) before ending with a rant about how messed up the world is because football players are paid £250k a week while benefits are being cut from those in need. Fair point Frank; if only there was some way of getting this inspirational singer-come-political ranter cleaned up and sent to the Houses of Parliament, he could probably have quite an impact and knock up a decent amount of support. It would make Prime Minister's questions far more watchable. However, he would never make it that far as this would likely destroy his far more important Busker's Got Talent career.

After an intriguing, political and musical bus journey, I hopped off at my stop and breathed in some lovely fresh London air, with the words "Hey! Teacher! Leave them kids alone!" ringing in my head.

Frank for Prime Minister! Looking forward to seeing you in Number 10 soon...

\<Dave Nomoney and Larry Odeur\>

While I embarked on my sixty-second walk to the bus stop, six buses whooshed past me. SIX!!! I've heard of the "You wait for ages and then three come at once," malarkey, but this was just obscene. SIX buses!!! Can you tell I was annoyed? Although, to be fair, when I finally did make it to the bus stop, I only had to wait two minutes for another one...

Later, as I walked through the depths of Waterloo underground station, I stumbled upon not just one, but two potential candidates to join Frank in Busker's Got Talent.

The first was at the bottom of the escalator. Let's call him 'Dave Nomoney'. He was tall with the stature and physique of a Flamingo and, to top it off, had green hair. A few piercings were spread around his nose, lips and ears. I think it is fair to say that his fashion sense is more commonly known in the homeless world as 'Oxfam-chic'. Don't ask me to explain this term, I'm no fashion expert. His audition consisted of a rendition of Razorlight's 'Golden Touch'. The guitar work was a bit sketchy but this was mainly because he was missing two strings. Considering this, and the droning background noise from the tube trains and bustling crowds, he wasn't half bad. I considered, for a moment, donating some money for his cause, but I was unfortunately stuck in the commuter lane. If I had stopped at this point, I would have caused major delays and disruption to other fellow commuters. There would have been crashes, honks, hoots, farts, frustration and annoyance. I couldn't face inflicting that on everyone. The chap in front of me, however, didn't seem to mind. It was carnage. As he stopped and bent down to drop some money into the hat, bags launched into the air, food went flying everywhere, shoes took off, and people were crashing into each other, falling like dominoes. The anger on people's faces, I mean crikey, it was glowing red around me. Taken from a bird's eye view, it must have been like seeing an army of red ants. The chap who had stopped and placed his change into Dave's collection hat, wandered on, utterly oblivious to the wreckage he had left behind him.

At the end of the travelator, I met the final candidate. This guy was a bit different. He seemed smart, elegant, hip in fact. So, I named him 'Larry Odeur'. He had dreadlocks, was wearing some relatively worn jeans and topped the whole ensemble off with a multi-coloured waistcoat. He was playing the saxophone and doing a little jig, getting really into it. I felt like dancing with him, he was *that* good.

Larry Odeur - a potential winner. Watch out for him on the new series of Busker's Got Talent, singing his own song entitled 'The Master of Twerking'.

<Hourly Rate>

Have you ever wondered how much a busker makes an hour? I certainly have.

I've lost count of the number of times I've walked past and always felt the need to look into the hat, bag, or piece of cloth that contains their collection of the day to tally the money. Obviously, when I say tally, I mean estimate. I don't want to linger too long, otherwise it may lead to having an awkward conversation. I can safely say I've never seen the paper form of treasure in there. Not even a fiver. It's always just loose change. I do feel slightly disheartened when you look and see three 1p coins. I know that any change is better than none, but 1p coins? Really? You think the busker is going to get anywhere in London with 3p? Even penny sweets are subject to inflation and probably now cost around 25p a pop.

Does a busker earn more than £15 for a day's work? If so, I guess it would be enough for a decent meal and a litre of white lightning or nice bottle of merlot, depending on the vices of that particular busker. You think your hourly rate is bad? Think about them the next time you walk on by.

So far I've come across the following buskers; guitarists, bassists, trombonists, saxophonists, recorder players, ukulele players, keyboard players, beatboxers and just good old fashioned solo singers. I reckon if a group of buskers got together and choreographed a musical routine, I'd definitely give them some money. I'm sure you would too right? They should seriously consider forming a super group and hitting

Busker's Got Talent on the nose. We all know that Frank is fantastic, so imagine how good the series would be with some other equally talented buskers. Diversity indeed. Their hourly rate would shoot up.

On a final note, while walking down the escalator one day, I heard a vague noise, which gradually increased in volume as I got closer to the bottom. Trying to make it out, my first thought was that the escalator was in fact breaking down. However, I soon realised that it wasn't the escalator, but some fella beatboxing; proper giving it some. He was coming out with the strangest of noises. Ridiculously, it sounded like an actual real music beat. How on earth was he making those kinds of noises? I was very tempted to join his act as a backing dancer, perhaps accompanying his beat by raving right in front of him (I'm sure that would help his earnings). That was, of course, until I realised that I would be the one boxed and beaten.

Stop 5: Easily Distracted

Woke up this morning. Blew nose (it is October after all). Brushed teeth. Sneezed on mirror. Wiped mirror. Showered. Ate toast (not in the shower). Locked flat. Crossed road (this can take as long as the shower part of the morning). Blew nose again. Caught the bus and a cute kid smiled at me. I realised in the reflection of the bus window that I still had snot coming down my nose. How attractive.

I arrived at Archway earlier than normal to try and make it to work early, but ended up being late as, inevitably, I had to wait 28 minutes for a tube via Charing Cross. It wasn't that there were delays, nope; just five trains whooshed past me. All of them were packed like penguins huddled together during a snowstorm in an episode of Planet Earth. I dread to think how stuffy it must have been on those tube trains that flew past. Why is it that some days the trains are all semi-full, boasting space, peace and uncongested, slightly healthier air, but other days they're completely and utterly rammed? There were no delays or part-suspensions or anything. Am I missing something or going mad?

After four stops on the tube, by some miracle, I obtained a seat and ended up next to an ultimate raver. He had what appeared to be a very expensive set of headphones on, but they certainly didn't keep his music in that's for sure. I was half expecting him to stand up, pull out the glow sticks and 'go all Ibiza!' on the rest of us (strong mental image). Sadly, this was not the case. Instead, I just sat there listening to some rather similar sounding bass beats. Normally when you hear other people's music you can at least attempt to participate in some amusement by playing the 'guess the tune game,' which is quite entertaining when it is something embarrassing like Justin Bieber or Steps. However, in this case, it was the classic, repetitive "du-du-du-du-du-du." It is distracting but what are you going to do? Ask him to turn it down? No chance. Just think of the looks you'd get...

Thanks to the loud music, I couldn't concentrate on reading a book or a newspaper. Searching for something – anything even – to make the journey pass quicker, I glanced up at the tube map. Ingeniously, it turns out that some juvenile with the same thirst for procrastination had spent their journey re-naming a couple of well-known stops on the map above the windows:

~~Bank~~ Wank.

(So original, nice one Connor, aged 8 from Brixton, you really don't appreciate those city-types, do you?)

My personal favourite:

~~Stockwell~~ Cockwell.

(Fantastic contribution there Timmy, I bet Stockwell feels overwhelmingly blessed by the originality of your stupendous change.)

How do they come up with these ideas? They really are true masters at work. The marketing industry needs to sign these people up. Otherwise it's just wasted talent.

I could not for the life of me stop thinking of rude names for other tube stations. I decided to join Connor and Timmy and have a go at re-naming some of them myself:

~~Bank~~ Wank.
(Ha! Just joking!)

~~Marylebone~~ Marksboner.
(Sorry Mark, I think that is even more immature than Connor and Timmy!)

~~Arsenal~~ Arse.
(That was too easy.)

Cockfosters.
(Hold on a minute... no need to change that one!)

What? It's not that easy to be original okay, you think you can do better? Answers on a postcode to:

[StamponYou]

1 Simply the Best
Betthanalrest
Betthananyone
NE1 13VERMET

And that was the end of my tube journey, wasting a total of 23 minutes thinking about funny rude names for tube stations... and failing miserably.

Pants. How productive.

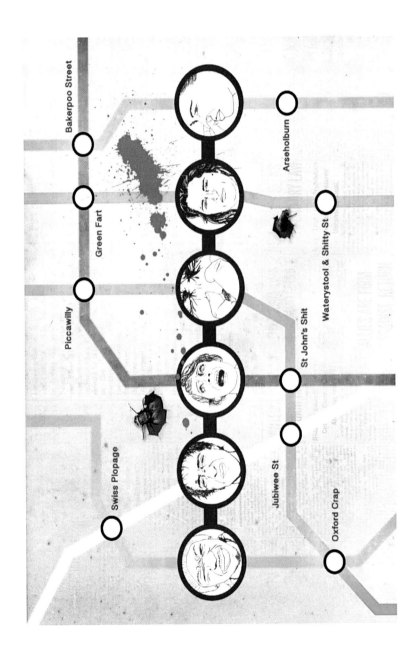

Bakerpoo Street

Green Fart

Piccawilly

Swiss Plopage

Arseholburn

Waterystool & Shitty St

St John's Shit

Jubiwee St

Oxford Crap

41

Stop 6: Advertising

Adverts on the tube can be quite effective, don't you think? Especially when you consider that a large majority of commuters have nothing to look at outside the window. Well, that's a lie. There is something. Blackness, followed by a blurred white wall every three minutes. Or, out of the other window – a sea of people. Anyway, my point is that us tube-goers don't have as much to look at compared to say the overground or bus commuters. They have the privilege of looking out into the world. Lucky buggers. I mean this might not be too pleasant if you are travelling through a highly polluted, murky, rat-infested backstreet, but at least you have the *option* to look outside.

Advertisers should see more potential in such an opportunity and gear their adverts specifically for us commuters as this isn't usually the case. For instance, I'm sorry, but we've all seen them – the large number of adverts about taking out short-term loans (that is – want cash now – get some) – up to £10k and it doesn't matter if you have a bad credit history (well, why would it?). As always I went straight to the small print hoping for comedy value. It did not fail me. The interest rate for repayment of a loan from this company was... wait for it... 700%. That's right, not 7%, not 70%, but 700%! I paused, considering the hilarity of it all, before realising that the people who are likely to sign up to this cruel payday-loan lending scheme are those that will fail to read the small print and ultimately end up being screwed.

Other notable adverts that I have seen on the tube are:

1)   Hair loss - I hope this isn't an indication as to the majority of people that commute every day.

2)   Bladder problems - see above. If this were the case, I'm *never* sitting down on the tube ever again. From here onwards I'll be known as the politest man on earth, always willing to give up any free seat.

3)   Broadband deals - I'm always a bit wary of some of the company names, such as "ROBU", "ScAmU" and "we'recrapdon'tbuybroadbandoffus LLP". It does get me a bit worried but what the hell, it only costs £4 a month. It's so cheap!

4)   Erectile disfunction - Err, probably not the best idea for people to take Viagra whilst commuting. Keep that bag on your lap sir!

5)   Dating websites - Quite ironic that if we, as a nation, had a more approachable attitude to public transport, Debbie wouldn't need to spend the £15 monthly subscription to find her match. She could simply go back to the old-school technique of meeting someone new by speaking (gasp!) to them on the tube (never!).

The most effective advert on my commute comes when I get off at Archway and walk towards the bus station, where there is a placard for a certain 99p cheeseburger. Seeing the advert five days a week, all year round, has really made me want to eat it. I do not go to the fast food chain that serves it very often, probably about once every two years. So, they are clever in their ways by putting a branch just three minutes from the advertising board. This means you don't have to travel particularly far to get your hands on one. I have managed to resist it so far, but the more I think about it... hold on...

(*munching noises*)

Yum, yum, yum. 99p. Totally worth it. Is there anything more tantalising than a juicy slab of grilled meat covered in melted cheesy goodness, coupled with crunchy iceberg lettuce, ketchup and mustard, in-between two nicely toasted buns (gherkins removed – controversial I know)? What a delight. Unless you're a vegan.

So, these adverts have now inspired me to think of something inventive for underground commuting. The first thing I need is a product to sell. Maybe something that can be used on the tube?

Drum roll please...

1) The Super Space Stick (SSS for short, not to be confused with the SS - crikey that would be bad!). This would be a mallet like the one Timmy Mallet had, of a sponge consistency, that can be used to hit people on the head so they get out of your way when you're in a rush. The upgraded

version could include a speaker that can be customised, for example, "Please, shove off, you're irritatingly slow."

Pros: Get to hit people, which helps with anger.

Cons: Encourages violence and you'll probably get arrested.

2)   Season ticket2. For just a small fee (£350,000 a year), you would gain access to a guaranteed heated seat with a free paper and coffee for your commute to work. Your name and face would be displayed on the seat. Anyone who incorrectly tries to sit in your reserved place would receive relentless electric shocks and be forced to listen to Barbie Girl on repeat for the remainder of their journey.

Pros: Travelling to work in style.

Cons: Fellow commuters will hate you.

So, the votes have been cast. Well, they haven't, I've just decided that the winner is...

Stop 7: Fashion Disasters

On a rather dark, damp morning, I had my head down and my coat wrapped around me nice and snug, in a desperate attempt to re-create the comfort and cosiness of my warm bed. I walked across from the bus stop to the tube station and could not help but notice a bright pink thong shining up at me. Now, this wasn't just the top of underwear that sometimes peeks up over the trousers when you're sitting awkwardly. The fact that I can tell you it was a thong I'm sure informs you how much of it was visible to the naked eye.

This *thing* made me wonder how on Earth the lady did not know/couldn't tell/didn't care that her underwear was so blatantly on show for everyone to see? For a start, it was freezing - Artic-like conditions. Considering she was dressed smartly and had a suit jacket on - one can only assume that she was going to work in an office environment. Bearing this in mind, how could she decide to wear trousers that didn't fit her properly and clearly displayed her underwear? This whole situation was leaving me very confused. Maybe this was a new hipster trend?

For all those noughties babes, guess which song popped into my head?

"That thong, thong, thong, thong thong."

Cheers Sisqo, thanks for that.

Incidentally, do you ever see something on the tube and it sparks a random memory from your past? Well, this did for me.

It made me think back to my teenage years when everything from a spot on your nose to someone else wearing the same t-shirt as you was the end of the world. I remember how the girls tried different methods of showing off just a hint of their bra. Whereas the guys wore hideously baggy trousers so that their boxers were constantly on show. There was also the growth of the culture of Emos, who brought with them the ingenious invention of wearing insanely tight trousers (with a belt), but *underneath* their bum. Therefore, any occasion that involved them lifting their hands up, crouching down, or simply leaning too far forward, meant we all got a nice flash of their bright green boxers. They also had a classic hairstyle; a lovely gelled fringe-y bit, you know what I mean:

Then there were the Chav girls, who would wear ludicrously tight tops and jeans. They were so constricted around their waists that their bellies would pop over the waistband and hang out for the world at large to see (more commonly known as 'muffin top'). In what way was that ever attractive, or more importantly, comfortable?

Looking back, I'm sure many of us had fashion disasters when we were younger that make us question – what on Earth was I thinking?!?

Yes, I will tell you mine; a side parting until I was 13 (Ha!), which once removed was then followed by consecutive summers of dyeing my hair blond. Also, I insisted on wearing one pair of baggy jeans for five years, even though each year they gained an additional hole somewhere. I felt like if I gave up on them, I'd have ruined my teenage years.

Note to self: always check myself in the mirror before leaving home. Oh, and download The Thong Song.

Stop 8: Merry Travelling

\<Classy Decorating\>

L ondon is starting to empty out for the festive period. My morning journey is becoming a tad less frantic and far more relaxed. I've managed to get a seat from Archway every morning this week, which is just completely unheard of (well, it's only Wednesday, but still, that's three mornings in a row). It's just beautiful, truly beautiful.

The same cannot be said for the Christmas lights in Archway. They look like they've been there every year since the 1800s. For those of you that have yet to experience the fantastic opportunity of visiting Archway at Christmas, please do go check them out. They are giant As. In fact, some of the bulbs in these As have completely lost their colouring, so are a rather unrelenting dirty white. And not to mention that some of the bulbs have blown and are still awaiting replacement. Brilliant. Nothing makes you feel more festive that that.

<Christmas Party>

It was the work Christmas party. I managed to drag myself away from the happening dance floor, where shapes were thrown, the splits were performed by a 50-year-old lady (no joke, very impressive) and the crab was attempted in response, but failed. I should have stayed longer, shouldn't I? When I'm next in work I am going to hear about my colleagues falling into their bosses and spewing everywhere, as well as hailing down a taxi aiming to get to Wimbledon, but ending up in Bethnal Green - easily confused.

In order to make the last train from London Bridge, which I just about managed, I took off at a brisk walking/near running pace. The underground at night is always an interesting sight, especially if it's the weekend. It was a Wednesday night though so I was thinking (stupidly perhaps) that it would be rather empty.

To my dismay, it was in fact more packed than at peak times, with all sorts (not of the liquorice variety) onboard. The vast majority consisted of high-class individuals wearing tuxedos/cocktail dresses in inebriated states. Some ladies had taken their six-inch heels off to reveal bruised, bloody and torn-up feet. The men had all undone their bowties and removed their jackets to reveal sprouting chest hair, beer bellies and damp patches around their armpits. Drunken stumbles followed as the train moved through the stations.

You know what is coming next don't you?

One lady, considerably more inebriated than anyone else, had been leaning against her male friend/work colleague for a while, with her hair flopped all over her face like Cousin IT from the Addams Family. She was barely able to stand up. Lots of leaning forward and to one side meant her male friend had to pretty much hold her up. We stopped at Camden Town and were delighted to see her chunder everywhere. Remember what I said about where her hair was? Lovely. I won't explain any further. Well, apart from the fact that there was a river filled with miniature boats slowly trickling its way down towards me and my fellow commuters. Surprisingly, I decided to move carriages.

As I was saying, these after-Christmas-party people (of which I was one), were joined by an array of other citizens on the tube, which included: the shift workers, the 'Jesus is with everyone' people and the normal 'Wednesday night' drinkers. These 'Wednesday night' drinkers were far more accustomed to the journey, obvious by the fact that they had bottles of water and snacks for the trip to help sober them up. Whereas the tux/cocktail dressers had kebabs, chips and the remains of red wine in plastic glasses, trying to continue the night in some fashion.

I stupidly went down the route of attempting to read my book, which I had been thoroughly enjoying for the last three weeks. Why? Why did I do this? All I can remember is looking at the pages and trying really hard to concentrate, but inevitably drifting off into unconsciousness, until I was rudely interrupted by the loud sound of chunder again at Archway.

Bleurgh.

\<Festive Joy\>

I reckon the population of London has decreased by about 66%* over this festive period (*complete guess). The tubes are empty. I've had so much room to myself that I've been putting my feet up, sometimes even lying down and reading the Metro with a cup of tea in my hand. Commutes should *always* be like this, it is wonderful.

Fellow commuters are far more relaxed and happy. A journey around this time could be described as... well... pleasant. Gasp! Even the bus and train drivers appear to be in a good mood; wearing Santa hats, festive jumpers or tacky tinsel. The tube drivers speak with more zing in their voice and some had cheerful comments to make when travelling on the Northern line. Here are a select few:

1) On approaching Tottenham Court Road– "Please alight here if you would like to join five million other people with their Christmas shopping."
2) When *trying* to leave Leicester Square– "Please can you remove your bags from blocking the doors; tablets and game consoles are expensive gifts, don't break them."
3) When leaving Kings Cross– "This train will be terminating at the North Pole."

If that doesn't make you smile in the morning, I don't know what would.

Talking about what makes people smile – the craze of the Christmas jumper seems to be spreading like wildfire. There are some utter classics everywhere. I was lucky enough to have my sister make me one with Rudolph sewn on the front; quite similar to the one Colin Firth wears in Bridget Jones. It brings joy to my fellow commuters when they see it, I have even seen a smile! Gasp!

Around London at the moment everything feels festive, which is joyous. I walked out of the chilly-willy weather and wandered into the side entrance of Waterloo (opposite the pub), where I was greeted by a large group of charity carol singers. They were good. So good that a large number of people had gathered around them with their phones out recording them sing. A couple of renditions of the classics even had the crowd joining in.

There is something about a large group of people who you don't know, joining together to sing, that really makes you feel warm inside, does it not? Whether it be at a gig, a sports match or even random carol singing, nothing beats a spontaneous rendition of "Santa Clause is coming to town" to get you in a festive mood.

Merry Christmas indeed.

Tube Announcement:

"Escalator out of order. Did you know that an escalator can also be used as a staircase?"

Stop 9: Cramped Conditions

<Wet>

Another great day of commuting for moi and thousands of other passengers. My journey began with a long wait at the bus stop in the pouring rain, my phone telling me that a bus had been due for the last ten minutes. If only I hadn't forgotten my umbrella and the bus shelter wasn't so busy. The kid next to me picked this exact moment to have a full on screaming match with her mum about an iPhone. The kid looked about six, and she was moaning about a phone, really?!? To the surprise of everyone at the bus stop, the mum screamed right back at her, at the top of her lungs. Sounded a bit like a dying cat. In a temporary state of bewilderment, I forgot who was the mum and who was the child in this argument. It all came to a rather abrupt end when the phone ended up on the floor in three bits. Cue further screaming.

Where's the friggin' bus I thought?!?

Straight on, squashed by the doors, tried to get my book out, accidentally knocked about three people, received one dirty look and a revenge fart aimed my way. It was one of those lingering, beer-to-egg smells that hung in the air, slowly making its way up my nose. RETCH.

PING!

One bus stop later, a lady squeezed past with a little munchkin, who decided to slap me on the arse on her way out (charming). Six more people forced their way on. One arm to the chin. Book fell out of my hands. Dammit! The amount of effort it was going to take to get my book back.

PING! PING! PING!

Next stop. People bundled off and my book was kicked outside into a large puddle. I quickly jumped off to grab it, but then the doors closed and the bus drove off. Today was going well wasn't it?

The nice fifteen-minute walk to the tube station left me well and truly drenched to the bone, with my hair stuck flat against my head. For the first time I realised that the shoes I was wearing must have had holes in them, as my socks were desperately damp. Every step produced very unpleasant squelching. No point reading my book as the pages were stuck together; it needed, like me, a good hair drying.

On reflection, I must have looked quite the sight as I stepped onto the tube. A proper drowned rat, with every individual part of me dripping. I'm sure that my fellow commuters wanted to stand in a cramped moving box with me by their side...

The lucky lady in red who was next to me, cheek to cheek, turned her head, took a good long look at the state of me, and then smiled. The train suddenly stopped and jerked, leading to me losing my balance and falling forward, showering her. The smile swiftly disappeared. I offered her my version of a towel, which was a tissue. Her smile re-appeared, with a quick laugh from both of us. I bet she'll never forget the way I looked that day.

Does a twenty-five-minute tube journey dry me off at all? Five minutes in, I wasn't expecting much. The rather uncomfortable feeling of being damp and wet, combined with the stuffiness of the train made me feel very sticky. The windows were steamed up and I wasn't sure what the drips on my forehead were, or the damp patches under my arm-pits (well okay, that was probably sweat). I felt a tiny amount of satisfaction when the guy who decided it was a good idea to squash on next to me, departed the train with his shirt dripping everywhere.

Face down with my nose pressed to the floor, I noticed a little puddle underneath me. Great. Now it looked like I'd well and truly wet myself. It slowly started to creep its way down the carriage...

\<Toxic Metro\>

Another packed day on the tube. Totally and utterly rammed.

The only inch of space came when we reached Goodge Street, where more than zero people got off. You could feel the whole carriage decompress, like the Chinese challenge for how many people you could fit in a Mini Cooper (see YouTube. Seriously, check it out). Hooray for space, not to mention that little pocket of extra oxygen allowing me to breathe normally. Oh, the delight of not having anyone nudge me in the back, accidentally hit me in the face with their book, or being forced to endure the stench of someone's smoky breath – never nice first thing in the morning. Today it was specifically the relief in no longer having to smell what seemed like toxic shampoo emitting from a lady's head. The smell was so distinct, so powerful; it wafted through the air like a group of bees, buzzing their way over and injecting my throat with the overwhelming sensation of nausea.

The only benefit in being so close to another person in this situation is when you've forgotten to pick up a Metro. If you're next to someone who is reading a copy, it's easy to peek over their shoulder and read it with them. Obviously, you have to read the stories quicker than you normally would, and sometimes they will skip past bits that you're interested in (such as, who got knocked out of the Bake Off last night, dammit!). The page could be turned at any second, so you are kept on your toes at all times (if you're not on your toes anyway, trying to read the paper).

I finally worked out why the train was so busy today – more Brexit-related protests. Apparently, people were off to the Houses of Parliament to start the...

(And then the guy turned the page over before I could finish reading.)

\<A City of Extremes\>

Busy, busy, busy; that's what they all say about London. Busy, busy, busy. Well, you know what? They're right.

From the bus, so unbelievably packed with men that I thought we were all being shipped off to war - to the tube - where I had to wait for three trains to get on. Tension was flying all over the place, hanging on every droplet and molecule of moist air, building up with every second. I could see the anger on people's faces. This would not be marked down as my most pleasurable commute. A little bit of back-chat here and there as a lady tried to get on at Kentish Town to remarks of:

"There's no room, don't be stupid."
"Would you all move down please?"
"Where? There's no room."

Rudeness came and went and the lady managed to find one third square metre of space to squeeze into so all was well with her. Well, apart from everyone else who were squeezed even tighter together.

Cue the popping sound of people's hernias coming out all at once.

Even the slightest of movements would lead to a delicate light pink umbrella - not even the knob end, but the spiky end - penetrating my nuts. I prayed to the tube gods that the train would run smoothly and that the driver was not a boy/girl racer. You know what I mean, the ones that harshly accelerate out of the blocks, followed by sharp, stiff braking. 'My nuts,' I prayed, 'think of my nuts Mr/Mrs Tube Driver.'

London is a place of extremes.

When I arrived at Waterloo (nuts intact, as I'm sure you'll be pleased to hear), the platform was unsurprisingly packed and it took around three minutes of shuffling to finally reach the top of the stairs. From there I made it to my favourite travellator and what was presented in front of me?

Complete, utter, emptiness.

I am not exaggerating. I could not believe my eyes as I failed to see even one person in front of or behind me. The travellator was broken, so I walked all the way down towards the exit, not encountering a single other human being. It was utter bliss. The only noise was the humming of the other travellator working away. I walked at my own pace, with my own space. It seemed so odd being able to find somewhere in central London at 9am on a Thursday morning where no other human being was. I thoroughly enjoyed every moment of that thirty-second walk.

Turns out the Jubilee line was part suspended and everyone was being held back at the barriers like cattle bursting before their twice daily milking. A sheer wall of over 100 people, all annoyed, frustrated and eager to get to work, were stood watching me with piercing eyes.

I strutted purposely out of the station towards a stunning clear blue skyline. I was fully appreciative of a journey that had begun so frustratingly, but which had somehow flip reversed into one of the more pleasant moments I had experienced on my commute into work.

With a large exhale of breath, relaxation of the shoulders and a beaming smile on my face, I walked off to fulfill my day's work (nuts still intact).

\<Brightening up the Day\>

Serious Monday morning blues; I think everyone was sharing it with me. I have never seen so many unhappy faces before.

Well, maybe apart from every other Monday on the tube.

I sympathise with everyone. After having such a lovely weekend, the last thing you want to do is get up on a dark and drizzly morning, where the wet autumn leaves have piled up and made the pavements hazardous. The minute you step out the door after you've just sorted yourself out to look half decent, a huge gust of wind blows leaves all over your face and dislodges your perfectly placed hair that had taken four precious morning-minutes. What a total waste of time. You'll look like a wreck by the time you get to the office.

Before:
Perfect hair

After:
Messed up hair (just look at the difference!)

Packing yourself into a confined space with hundreds of other miserable commuters who have more than likely had a very similar start to their morning is not 'the dream'.

Thankfully, one thing did lighten my mood and coaxed out just a hint of a smile on a dreary and depressing Monday. This was someone who I decided to name 'Polar Bear Woman'. She boarded the train at Mornington Crescent and boy did she stand out.

Right, let's start from the bottom upwards (not in a rude way - cheeky!). She was wearing clean and crisp white UGG boots (obviously brand new), followed by bright white, thick knee-length socks, which she complimented with white linen trousers that were tucked *into* the socks. This ensemble was finished off with a long, white fluffy coat. For a minute I was concerned that this may have been a real polar bear (not alive, obviously, just skinned for the fur). However, when I relayed my concerns to my girlfriend later that night, she helped dislodge this worried assumption of mine by saying that apparently polar bear fur isn't white. Who would think it?

The fact is - polar bear fur is transparent; it has no colour. Polar bears look white because of the way their fur reflects visible light. Of course, looking white helps a polar bear blend right into the ice and snow. Phew! Thank god for that. No polar bears were harmed writing this segment.

But yes, anyway, as I was saying... where was I? Oh yes, the Polar Bear Woman. She stood out and brightened up my Monday morning - literally. To say she received a few odd looks on my journey is a massive understatement.

I was mainly worried about the man standing next to her, holding a coffee, who didn't look very stable on his feet... just think of that dry-cleaning bill!

<Luckless>

You realise it's not your day when you reach the bus stop and three fly past, leaving you with a ten-minute wait in the rain. When you finally manage to get on the bus, this is then kindly followed by a twelve-minute delay at one stop for no apparent reason.

Your luck has totally run out for the week when every traffic light that you want to walk through turns against you, leaving you waiting on the pavement for a green man to appear. I tried to tell myself this should be the end of it, bad luck comes and goes, so I should be back to evens in no time. I'd leave it like that and try my upmost to not feel aggrieved.

However, I pottered into the station and saw on the information board that my train was leaving now or in twelve minutes. Well, I'm not making the train that leaves now, so no need to rush. I stood on the escalator and walked casually down the stairs, only to see the doors close and my train leave the instant I placed my foot on the platform. Ah well, I'll just get the next train to Camden and change there.

I arrived at Camden and briskly walked to the other platform (casual walking obviously wasn't sufficient today). I reached the top of the steps and saw another Charing Cross train swiftly leaving the platform the minute my foot hit the floor. Crikey, do the trains see me as some kind of predator? I'm not a lion, although my star sign is Leo and my hair is a bit bushy, but that's not the point. A lion wouldn't be a predator to an underground train anyways. It would get crushed. Fact.

It just wasn't going to be my day as even on this platform I had to wait seven minutes for another train. When I finally got on, every person around me was getting off so that seats were instantly taken. Except for the two people in front and behind me of course, who, typically, were like me – on the train all the way to Waterloo.

I seemed to be in the way of every person on the train, constantly getting knocked on the shoulder, stamped on the foot, or a wayward bag slung into the middle of my face with a perfect connection.

To even it out, there was a turnaround of luck that evening when I played poker against some friends and won £30. Not that I am saying that poker is a game of luck or anything... but maybe I should have invested in a lottery ticket instead.

IT COULD BE YOU.

\<Hot Stuff\>

So, I've heard that commuting on the Central Line isn't fun. I thought the Northern Line was busy enough, but apparently, I was *very* wrong. Several friends warned me but I thought they were just exaggerating. They really weren't.

I'd done my duty of being a nice, thoughtful boyfriend and had bought two tickets to a gig in Shepherds Bush for my girlfriend and I. My trek began by travelling on the Northern Line towards Bank to change onto the Central line.

My
Oh
My

They are not lying; it really is busy (understatement), and hot (double understatement). The air was dry and humid, almost dirty, and I could tell the instant I managed to catch a train heading for Shepherds Bush (with my face plastered against the glass, steaming up the doors), that this wasn't going to be a pleasant experience. Everyone on the carriage was dripping, so much so that you could see wet patches under armpits, combined with traces of sweat covering foreheads. I imagine it felt something like the Sahara, although I've never been so maybe I'll stick with something I can compare it to - sitting in a sauna with a hangover. I can safely say that it was the most uncomfortable tube journey I've *ever* been on. I had a renewed appreciation for clean, fresh air and any kind of personal space. At least the trains were coming through every two minutes. I can't imagine how bad it would be if the line went down.

I arrived at Shepherds Bush and was exceptionally relieved to be above ground, with some fresh (well, London-fresh) air and much needed personal space (well, London-personal-space). After that journey, I needed a good hosing down to clean all the grime and sweat off me. My shirt was a mess. I knew I shouldn't have chosen a light colour...

The gig was *cough* will Young *cough*. We were stood about six rows back from the front (quite a good view), and had the momentous luck of being positioned behind a completely drunk, crazy-for-Will fan. Whenever Will (we are best mates now, so I can refer to him as Will) sang a calm song, she would screech with drunken purpose and intent:

"I love you Will!". Quickly followed by
"Wiiiiiiiiiiiiiiiiiiiiiiiiiiiiiiiiiiiiiiiiiiiiiiiiiiiiiiiiiiilllllllll!".
Then
"I've taken my bra off for you Will."

We restrained ourselves from letting her know that he wouldn't be interested - mainly because she probably didn't care, wouldn't have heard us or was just too damn drunk. She continued to dance ferociously, which often ended up with her crashing into the chap in front of me, who wasn't at all impressed. Poor guy. We spent the remainder of the evening praying that she didn't spew everywhere.

At one point, she looked on the edge and I thought to myself, "I think I better leave right now." But I didn't.

Stop 10: Teenage Antics

C hav central today. I was travelling from Southwark to Victoria on my way home to Sussex for New Year's. Some fellow passengers and I were treated to a ridiculous conversation that had started between two teenage girls. The girls, both 13 (I managed to deduce this from their discussion), were sat next to each other and right by them was a lovely elderly couple. I was seated diagonally opposite.

The girls both had some interesting fashion sense and, like all chavs, wore very tacky-fake-looking gold jewellery. Their hair was tied up as tightly as humanly possible on the back of their heads. Ouch!

Their antics began with them partaking in some kind of dance routine that they appeared to have learnt from a music video. We were also lucky enough to be treated to some lyrics they sung to go with it (I'm too out of touch to know who or what is cool anymore – Skepta?). This was all harmless enough, some might even say slightly entertaining and amusing. They certainly found it hilarious and were obviously enjoying it.

Following this came the masterpiece, some may say the main event. It was a delightful conversation that went a little like this (note – obviously I've made up the names - I don't know them):

> **Rudy**: So, you got a man on the go at the mo?
> **Lisa Left-Eye**: Yeah, he's 17.
> **Rudy**: But you're only 13! What's he like?
> **Lisa Left-Eye**: I know, but who cares? He's mint, got a massive c*** too.
> **Rudy**: Have you done stuff with him then?
> **Lisa Left-Eye**: Yeah, like everything innit.
> **Rudy**: Yeah, same with my man, he's only 15 though.
> **Lisa Left-Eye**: Got a small d***?
> **Rudy**: Well yeah, he's only 15, but it's alright.
> **Lisa Left-Eye**: It's all about size.
> **Rudy**: Yeah, defo, 100%.
> **Lisa Left-Eye**: He's even c** on my chest.
> **Rudy**: You what? That's mingin'.
> **Lisa Left-Eye**: Nah, it's proper sexy like.

Sorry, what?!? Who talks about this in public?

At this point, I looked over at the elderly couple sitting next to them, anticipating some rather shocked and horrified looks. Surprisingly, they were, like me, smiling and failing miserably to contain their laughter. It was obvious by the way the girls were talking that they had never done anything with a guy and were just trying to look cool in front of each other and show off.

A fantastic way to end the day on a tube, with some light-hearted, typical new-age British entertainment. Shutdown.

Stop 11: Rap it Out

I do love the emergence of a random event that spices up an otherwise dull and routine journey. Today was one of those instances and it was particularly spontaneous.

It was during rush hour, and the tube was fully packed to the brim as usual. I looked around and knew that everyone had the same intention – they wanted to be off this stuffy, cramped carriage and be at home with a cold beverage in hand watching Masterchef. Nope. Not yet. I still had a good hour of travelling before I would reach that haven. Suck it up.

So, I scrambled into the only square metre of space available. Next to me was a tall black man; young, looking cool, wearing baggy jeans and a cap.

Out of nowhere, he started aggressively rapping at speed and, to be honest, it was a lyrical dream. The rhymes that he threw into the mix were Another Level. I thought to myself – THIS is raw talent. Obviously every commuter instantly turned the other way, trying to ignore him.

A suited and booted older man (one of those snobby city types) was standing face-to-face with the rapper and looked exceptionally embarrassed as he tried his best to avoid eye contact. Due to the cramped conditions, there was just nowhere to look because he couldn't move his head. The rap continued for one seemingly longer-than-usual stop.

After finishing on a particularly strong beat, he introduced himself and opened up shop with CDs to sell. He received no response, probably for several reasons:

1) His approach scared the living daylights out of everyone on the carriage.
2) This was probably not the right time or place to introduce his music to the world; on a commuter train full of people whose top priority was getting home.
3) The conditions were cramped. It didn't make any sense to try and open a music store on the carriage, where people would likely cause more disruption to the journey by digging into their pockets and buying CDs.

For me though, it was nice to see and hear something different on my journey home. I would have bought his CD, if only I had a CD player at home... What is this, the 90s?

It left me wondering if he would rap again to the new people that got onto the carriage – maybe they would be a more captive audience and join in?

Perhaps tonight Mr Rapper, you never know, they may want to get freaky with you?

Stop 12: Under the Influence

<Salesman Dave>

I traipsed down the stairs of my flat into the ~~beautiful sunshine~~ dark, damp, extremely windy morning. Yaaay, fun times.

I made it to the bus stop with half my head blown off, eyes watering from the wind's almighty force. Thank god for the person who invented a three-sided bus stop, which provided me with some respite from the dreadful weather.

I was greeted by an over-eager looking male (his eyes reminded me of someone on Coke; and I don't mean the beverage), who I called 'Salesman Coke Dave'. He proceeded to ask me continuous questions that started with "Are the sales still on?" and ended with a sales pitch about how awesome this shop on Oxford Street was and how much he recommended that I visit it. I offered him the standard commuter nod and thought to myself:

1) I am going to work this morning, I don't get up this early to go shopping.
2) I have £20 left in my current account to last me the whole of January, I don't think a new t-shirt with 'LEG' on the front and 'END' on the back is my top priority.
3) I'm not sure it's a smart idea to take recommendations off a man who I'm 95% sure is currently on Coke, if not, some other terrible drug.

I didn't have the heart to tell him any of this, so in true commuter fashion, I legged it onto the bus and immediately locked onto a spare seat.

Phew, I had managed to escape his crafty salesmanship. Not so lucky for others though. All I could hear for the remainder of my bus journey was him using the same routine on a poor old lady, who was caught unaware, too late in realising his ploy. This meant no escape for her until we reached Archway. I've never seen anyone (not even Usain) bolt (excuse the pun) so fast off a bus before; she was like Speedy Gonzalez. Arriba, Arriba.

On the upside, at least Salesman Coke Dave took my mind off the dreaded January blues (cue "Holidays are coming, holidays are coming," going around my head, 11 months early).

\<The White Stuff\>

So, it was mid-afternoon on a Saturday and my girlfriend and I were on the tube from South Kensington to Kings Cross. We were greeted by a drunk, stocky man, early 20s, *pretending* to throw up everywhere. When I say pretending, he was just hurling and doing an incredibly poor acting job. I thought to myself, I could do far, far better than this guy, he's pants! Call that vomiting?!?

He then proceeded to start running up and down the carriage, almost as if he'd heard me, pretending to throw up on every person sitting down. To be fair, he was improving and his mates were loving it. However, as always, my fellow commuters didn't let me down - everyone ignored him, looking down or blankly ahead. His acting was obviously that pathetic that nobody gave a rat's arse - I certainly didn't. He wouldn't be winning a BAFTA anytime soon, that's for sure.

Following this, he decided it would be hilarious to annoy a young guy who was asleep. It started with a little nudge, then a shout of "Oi!" in his face, then a tap on his leg, nose and forehead combined with the retching sound. That was the ticket. The guy woke up with a jolt, his bloodshot eyes wide open. There was a lot of hand shaking and a bit of drunken chat, although unfortunately we couldn't hear any of what they were conversing about.

The sleepy guy stood up to get off at the next stop; would you believe what he did next? He looked, lurched his face forwards and pretended to throw up! A hell of a lot of laughter from the group ensued, alongside the chanting of "Legend, Legend, Legend."

Well, that was quite enough for one journey, or so you'd think...

After these antics, some seats became available next to two young guys in their twenties, who also looked extremely inebriated. A bit of playful pushing and shoving started between them with some mumbled, incomprehensible chat. My initial concern was the possibility of a fight. One of the guys got the other into a headlock and was rubbing his head, messing his hair up (never a good thing to do to a man who looked like he was from hipster Hackney). I felt apprehensive as to what would follow. Well, it was definitely unexpected.

Coke.

Can you believe that on public transport in the middle of the afternoon?

Coke.

To apologise for the headlock, his friend casually (as you do every day on the tube, right?) pulled out a clear plastic bag and sprinkled some white powder onto the guy's hand.

Snort. Snort.

Finger to the nose to sniff all the remnants up.

Snort. Snort.

Why not another line? There's only the whole tube watching. I cannot put into words the expressions on fellow passengers faces.

One last line before we get off? Why not? It is a Saturday afternoon on the tube, classic Coke'a'clock.

Snort. Snort. Shake of the head.

They stood up to get off and one of them dropped the remainder of the bag onto the floor. He looked up and proclaimed to the carriage, "A bit early, but Merry Christmas everyone," as he stumbled out of the doors and nearly took someone out on the way.

We were all treated to an early snowstorm. Holidays are coming.

\<Tube Hangovers\>

Man alive. Being hungover on a tube journey to work is not fun. Not fun at all. Man alive. Urgggggggggggh.

It's always the "I'll stay for one more" problem when it comes to work drinks. Once you've had that one more, and subsequently many more after that (coupled with not eating anything), you soon forget that you have work the next day. Pants.

Everything seems to take longer and is considerably louder. You can't sort your body temperature out – it's too hot in here, better take the jacket off. What?! Sweet Jesus its cold in here, let's put the jacket back on. On. Off. Too cold. Too hot.

The bus was rammed. It was obvious to fellow passengers that I was struggling. Too much drink, not enough sleep; this teamed with the potent smell of sweat did not help my reflux. My head was pounding with the sound of a baby crying.

What followed was a motion that I didn't realise would be particularly painful – the escalator to the tube, as it chugged along (similar to a bad gear change in a car). It played havoc with my stomach.

A guy standing next to me on the tube carriage started chewing gum, 'Squelch, slurp, chew, chew.' All I heard was the sound of his deafening saliva. Like a shitty One Direction song you spend your life trying to tune-out, it repeated very loudly and profoundly in my head. 'Chew, chew, chew. Slurp. Gulp.'

Ahhhh!

As we approached Tufnell Park, "The next station is Tufnell Park," blurted out over the tannoy. It was just **so** loud. **So, so loud.** Why? Pain.

Then came another motion, as the pace of the train increased, followed by a little jolt, acceleration, jolt, acceleration, jolt, acceleration, jolt. I wondered if I was going to survive this. Like a novice sailor, the increasing swell of the engine rocked my body back and forth. Back and forth. Back and forth. I concentrated profusely on trying to keep my balance and mind off the obvious. Acceleration, jolt, acceleration, jolt, slow down, sharp brake. Acceleration, jolt.

I grabbed a seat but, despite my greatest hopes of resolution, this didn't improve things. As I no longer needed to concentrate on keeping my balance, all I could think about was trying to think of something to think of. This just ended up with me thinking of the one thing I was trying to not think of.

Acceleration, jolt, acceleration, jolt. Please sweet Mary Jesus of the train gods. Let. This. End.

"The train is now approaching Mornington Crescent."

Noooooo, there were still so many stops to go. Urgh.

The lady next to me began fidgeting like a dog on heat seeing his bitch for the first time. Non-stop fidgeting. She just could not sit still. It's like she'd gone cold turkey or something. Seriously, she needed to sit still.

People surely couldn't get more annoying? Oh no, wait a minute, of course they could! Enter a chap who decided to bring breakfast from a popular fast food chain on board. Cheers for that. The fumes from the sausage, bacon and egg muffin started to make their way through the carriage and I sniffed the wonders of a breakfast far superior than the meagre buttered toast that I had eaten earlier that morning. My stomach churned and started to rumble, my mouth ached for salted food. What I would have given for one of those.

As the train journey neared its end, I realised how unbelievably thirsty I was. I opened my bag to locate my filtered water bottle (posh I know but London water is disgusting), only to discover that it was empty as it had leaked all over my bag. How wonderful. Right. That was it. I escaped to the nearest well known fast food establishment.

I promised myself I would never drink on a work night **ever** again (famous last words)... until next week.

Stop 13: Olympic Travelling

<Opening Ceremony>

The day had finally arrived.

"Tottenham Court Road station is now open to Northern line trains."

After eight months on the Northern line, with every journey sporadically interrupted by the announcement of "This train will not be stopping at Tottenham Court Road," the station that I only associated with a silver wall was now... another stop added to my journey.

The train pulled into Tottenham Court Road and I waited in anticipation to see the 'new look' station in all its glory. A total of four people departed. Three others looked in astonishment (obviously having paid no attention to any previous announcements) and then made a last desperate dive for the doors. In my mind, this played out like a famous Tom Daley dive, performed by the three people in total synchronisation. It looked so well executed, they should compete in the Olympics. If only 'Underground Tube Diving' was a recognised Olympic sport, I'm sure quite a few of us Londoners would be great at it. If Bowls can make it into the Olympics – why not this?

You'll be pleased to know that everyone made it off with all limbs intact, apart from one chap. His foot got trapped in the doors, and through the sheer force of his dive, it dramatically tore apart from his leg. There was blood everywhere, tendons strewn all over the floor and a lonely looking foot on the train by itself...

NOT!!!

I assume that gave you a dire mental image. To help remove that from your brain, try thinking of something completely different. For example, a beautiful sandy beach with an aqua blue sea and... giant cockroaches crawling out of the sand and happily munching on your feet! Sorry, just think about otters, they're great.

Anyway, I diverge.

After these people left the train, I took the opportunity to look at the new magnificent station. There were bare walls made from stone with dirt and cracks everywhere. Obviously this had been purposely modified to make it look 'rustic', 'artisan' or something similarly-hipster.

Remarkably, TfL said it would be ready by late November and, what do you know, it was ready *on time*. The same can't be said for when they built the new Wembley Stadium or Crossrail...

Hooray! I finally had access to the Central line to experience a furnace of hell. There was even a TV crew on the platform when the train flew past, interviewing someone about how great the upgrade was no doubt.

(**Note to self**: DO NOT tune into the local London news tonight to see that insightful segment.)

My only real concern with this re-opening was a consideration that is essential to any commuter - would it cause further disruption to my commute (that is, would my journey now take longer to complete and would the conditions be even more cramped?)

If not, wonderful.

If yes, HELL ON TOAST WITH BEANS, OREGANO, SLICED CHEESE AND MAYBE A DROP OF LEA AND PERRINS.

\<Language Barrier\>

I first became aware of how the London Olympics would affect my commute from an announcement by a hilarious old toff, whose insultingly posh Oxford accent boomed over my bus' tannoy:

Tannoy

"Londoners, this is your Mayor of London, Boris here. I hope you're having a lovely commute. I thought I would give you a little warning that some extra people will be using the transport system around London over the next few weeks. It may lead to you all having to queue for tubes as if they were rollercoaster rides; so to add to the excitement of when you get on a train or bus, we're going to increase the speeds to 120mph. We'll also take a delightful picture of you between each stop, and then try and flog it to you as an Olympic experience. We'll have key-rings, mugs, caps, t-shirts and many more things on offer. Oh, and before I go, we're turning off all fans and lights to save electricity. Toodles."

(Please note: This is a slightly adjusted prose from the original.)

When we (I say we, I cannot claim any responsibility) were hosting the world's largest sporting event, did we really expect zero disruptions? I was just happy that the tube didn't break down.

So arrived the tourists, stumbling into the city in their bucket loads. My journey back one evening was dominated by foreign languages.

First came the Spanish. Jesus can they speak el rapido. I took Spanish GCSE and managed to grab a B thanks to a pretty awesome teacher but what can I remember?

"Me gustaria el San Miguel."

Well, maybe a little bit more than that, which is why I tried to listen in to the conversation and grasp what they were chatting about. They spoke so quickly that by the time I understood one of the words, they'd finished talking and had started speaking in English.

Imagine what the English language would sound like if we sped it up, say x5 (for example, try doing so with a programme you've recorded on TV).

Exactly. It would sound crazy.

Next, I was treated to a group of American teenage girls (not technically a foreign language, I know, but they've altered so many perfectly fine English words, I wouldn't hold it against anyone for thinking so). They were delightfully well-spoken and eloquent. I think my ear-drums burst in-between Kentish Town and Tufnell Park.

At least they smiled a lot, which is always a pleasant surprise as the average commuter doesn't know what a smile is. Although, if everyone spoke at the same level of decibels, we'd all become deaf very quickly (perhaps this is why they are so chirpy - you cannot hear all the bullshit through the inaudible decibels).

My evening commute ended in Germany, that's right, Deutschland! Some say it's a brutal and unattractive language. Maybe. I prefer to think of it as efficient and to the point. There's no messing around when it comes to Deutsch talk.

I'll admit that it does sound the most aggressive out of any language I've come across, well, that or the guys on the tube were having an argument. Actually, that would make sense as they didn't part on the best of terms: with one of them hitting the other with a pepperoni. As one left the train, the other placed his hanky on the empty seat. When questioned about it, he simply replied "My friend will return, he put this down this morning at the crack of dawn."

<Olympic Reject>

I think someone failed to make the GB team for the Olympics but can't admit it to themselves. I had just sat down for my lovely commute home from Waterloo and the doors made that 'ding, ding, ding' noise as a warning that they were closing. (That is, don't try and get on because it will lead to certain injury or you looking like an idiot.) I'd really like to know the stats of how many people get things stuck in the doors every year. I can only assume that hundreds of phones, bags or other high value items are broken on an annual basis.

Anyway, I caught this Olympic reject out of the corner of my eye as she ran onto the platform and then tried to re-create a scene from a James Bond movie. She jumped as if she was a long jumper. Her leap was impressive.

She made it.

Shame her husband struggling with all the luggage did not.

He was left standing, a lonely soul, probably questioning his wife's motives when she only had to wait two minutes for the next one.

Well, would you believe it: at the very next stop (Embankment), someone tried the same thing? This time they didn't pull it off. His leg was stuck in the door. Ouch. Half of me felt pity for the pain he was in, but then the other half (actually, more like 80%) thought: stupid, stupid man.

Tannoy

"This is your conductor speaking, I'd just like to take this opportunity to remind passengers to keep their belongings and clothing clear of the doors, this includes any trailing limbs."

While he was stuck and didn't make it onto the carriage, an athletic rat that had been wandering around the platform did make a successful leap. He'd obviously decided that the northbound service to High Barnet was the right train for him (I don't think the passengers screeching on the carriage agreed).

<Gold>

On the penultimate day of Olympic travelling, I felt inspired and decided to run to work, all 14.4km. Really? A 14.4km run? Don't think so.

I did run about 300 metres to the bus as I was a little late, but man that took it out of me; there was lots of huffing and puffing. After an epic ten-minute bus journey, I then powered my way through another 200 metres to reach the platform. I was in 3rd place after all the people getting off the bus, behind a Chinese man and a Polish lady. It was pretty tight for the last few metres to the barrier until I got tipped (shoved) as I tried to get through. Next stage, the tube.

I was gearing myself up for a crazy busy journey... train pulled in... empty. Probably about 30% full, so not a herculean effort to find a seat. Meanwhile, a chap from Australia was disqualified for spitting on the platform (train conductor announced his disqualification). He could face a lengthy ban.

It's all about pacing yourself. A few stragglers dropped off at Highgate and Archway, having gone out too fast, cramping up from the fast-paced run to the bus.

Euston and Warren Street appeared and people collapsed under the pressure, falling asleep everywhere. By the time we reached Leicester Square there were only five competitors I could spot from the original starting line-up.

Before pulling into Waterloo, I performed my trademark stretches: side oblique, crescent pose, downward dog, beer squat twist. I was anticipating madness when I reached

Waterloo, warming up for lots of ducking and diving in and around people.

It was deafeningly quiet. It was like how I'd always want to travel around London, with about half the amount of people. And, to top it all, it made my race for the finish line even easier. When I reached the last escalator, there was nobody in sight, absolutely no one. So much for the insane amount of people and extra queuing that we were scare-mongered into believing by Boris and the media.

More importantly, I beat my fellow commuters, to clinch the gold medal (really it was a gold chocolate coin that I bought myself to celebrate, with my own money).

\<Rule Break Exception\>

With the Olympics in full swing, London was volunteer central for a couple of weeks. Everywhere I looked there was someone in bright pink, desperately searching for the people of Britain, to encourage them to donate their coffee money for the greater cause. Apparently, there were over 15,000 volunteers; nothing beats a bit of free labour.

Unfortunately, as with many good things, the Olympics eventually came to an end. I experienced an issue-free, efficient and extremely slick tube service the whole time. I even got to park my behind on a seat every day and spent most of my journeys high-fiving volunteers and anybody donning GB attire. Now *that* is what commuting should be like.

I chatted to people on the tube, I repeat, *chatted* to people, on the tube! That's a breach of Commuter Rule 1. Whoops!

I was even lucky enough to attend two events:

1) Olympic rowing at Eton Dorney, where I witnessed our first gold medals. COME ON TEAM GB!
2) Paralympic athletics, where I visited the incredible Olympic stadium, which is now forever blowing bubbles.

Overall, the whole Olympic atmosphere had an extremely positive effect on me. The most important thing is to keep that positivity going.

Two weeks later – everyone was miserable again.

Tube Announcement:

"The author is regulating (quickly writing) the next chapter. Normal service will resume shortly."

Stop 14: Hostile Attitudes

\<Accidental Offences\>

I picked up a Metro outside Archway station for the first time in about five months. Bored with books, I hoped this new reading material would provide some light entertainment for my commute to work.

As I plodded on down the escalators to the platform, I remembered why I gave up reading the Metro. Tube trains are packed, so trying to read a paper, or even trying to turn the page, becomes an art form. You need skill and agility to do so in such cramped and confined spaces. I was obviously out of practice, a little rusty, and so ended up (not purposely), hitting people everywhere when attempting to turn each page. I was *that* annoying human, a constant irritant. I tried my best, even waited for the train to stop and for people to get out before I attempted to read the other side of the page. Inevitably, with all the jerky movements, I still managed to stroke the back of someone's head (creepy!) or knock their glasses off somehow.

I also realised how little writing there is in the Metro, as I ended up having to turn pages every 10 seconds or so. Folding them in half, then half again, putting lots of effort into finding a spot where I could read about how a giant elephant saved a baby monkey from being eaten by a leprechaun or something similar.

Finally, the train emptied out so by the time I reached Charing Cross, I had space to read and turn pages at my leisure. I left my copy of the Metro in the recycling bin at the station. Do it. Don't be lazy and leave it behind your seat, on the escalators by that sign that sticks out, or just on the benches where people sit to wait for a tube.

David Attenborough is watching.

\<The Snake Pit\>

When I walked down the escalator, I was greeted by a wall of human beings on the northbound platform for the Northern line. It was packed to breaking point with a four-person-wide queue that snaked around the corner. Several people pushed past to reach the platform, before working out that we were all queueing for the same thing (shockingly). What ensued were a myriad of the Great British expletives, which included lots of "For f***'* sake", and "s***, b******, boob, f***, penis." All performed with venom in a variety of accents by my fellow commuters.

People do seem to enjoy other's misery. Some commuters slipping off the trains were laughing, pointing and joking about those who were queuing and suffering with the delays. Laughing? Really? Hiss off.

I know that not being a part of such a horrifically cramped, constricted and long journey ahead is a relief, but laughing is harsh. Karma will come back to bite them in the behind.

The only way I can begin to imagine why people would act with such severe potency was that it must be like driving on a motorway. For example, you're cruising along in your Shelby Cobra and you notice that everyone on the other side is crawling along at 3mph in terrible traffic. Whereas there you are speeding through at 70mph with no delay. All you can think is thank god that isn't me over there. Totally understandable response, but no laughing please. Viper that smirk off your face.

Back on the platform, my train of thought led me to the conclusion that this would be a perfect time to start a sing song to entertain all the bored, frustrated commuters. I could get a pungi out and start charming everyone with a rendition of Bruce Springsteen's 'Born to run', where the chorus line is changed to:

"Baby, we were born to
queuuuuuuuuuuuuuuuuuuuuuuuuuuuueeeeeeeeeeeeeeeeeeeeeee,
dur, dur, dur, dur.
Duuuur, duur."

This only happened in my head but it received quite the reception.

\<Personality Change\>

For the first time since I started documenting my tube experiences, I noticed a young lady on the train with a beaming smile. I repeat, **a beaming smile**. This must have meant one of two things:

1) It was her last ever journey on the tube or:
2) It was her first.

This got me thinking to back in the day, when I undertook my first proper commuter journey to London.

June 2010. The sun was shining, the birds were singing (some form of Bohemian Rhapsody but I couldn't be 100% sure) and all was wonderful with the world. I walked up to the tiny platform at Littlehaven station (a small, rather more traditional railway station next to a popular commuter town), where my train was due in three minutes. The voice on the tannoy was cheerful and pleasantly happy. Everyone was polite and smiling (well that is what I remember from my distorted memory) and I easily got a window seat and a lovely view of the Sussex countryside. I even had time to read a substantial amount of my book (Mr. Men: I highly recommend it, lots of pictures). All was well with life.

The important question to ask is, where did it all go wrong? Feel free to add to my non-exhaustive list:

1) Delays. Delays. More delays.
2) Smelly trains.
3) Rude humans.
4) Commuting in the winter (cold, dark and depressing).
5) Commuting in the summer (hot, sweaty and stuffy).
6) Commuting into or around London – this includes the journeys where you face huge quantities of fellow travellers around you: in your face, sitting on you, falling on you, cutting you up, coughing on you, sneezing on you, dropping food on you, sleeping on you, 'accidentally' knocking into you, talking too loudly, listening to music too loudly, eating stinky food around you, being on the phone around you. Don't stop me now... I could go on.

Everyone who commutes for a substantial amount of time (anything over a year) knows what I'm talking about. It has a talent of just creeping up on you before you even notice it, and suddenly you become 'one of them'. It's a kind of magic (but not the good stuff).

This is all thanks to the everyday routine that involves a constant struggle to get to work, in minimal time, under pressure, with the least disruption. The attitude of your fellow human beings rubs off on you and it can be difficult to break free. You get in that mode and if something or someone dislodges or interrupts the way in which your commute should take place, then suddenly the world is full of idiots and you end up becoming a miserable git. Everything and everyone is then out to get you and consequently you must now scowl all the time, push past people and tut a lot. These are the Commuter Rules. It is the way.

<Don't look back in anger>

I think that there is an imaginary force at the card barriers. This unknown force, that we cannot see, transforms the moods of people that walk through it. People change from half-decent, polite, respectable human beings into selfish, fast-paced, angry, unemotional individuals. Frustration and anger are the only 'acceptable' feelings allowed.

From the moment you swipe the card reader, your personality changes. It's as if you know what is coming next and you must mentally prepare yourself for any possible event.

This must be the reason why something happened on my journey back from work that I couldn't ignore. I missed the Mill Hill East train by roughly around half a second. The next train wasn't for another six minutes, so I decided I would get the earlier one to Edgware (due in a minute - waiting six minutes is just too much for me!) and change at Camden instead.

The train was comfortably empty, nothing was going on and this was exactly what I wanted from my commute home. Fifteen minutes later, I casually nipped off at Camden and skillfully dodged my way across platforms to the High Barnet branch, where a train was due in one minute. (So proud of myself saving five entire minutes of waiting time – what commuter skills!)

The train slowly crawled to the platform and from a first glance it looked busy. I had my fingers crossed everyone would get off here. The doors opened and I obeyed Commuter

Rule 3, letting people off the train first, which a man on the other side was also doing. I then proceeded to walk on and took a glance behind me, where the rule-abiding man was standing back to let a latecomer off the train first. He then stepped onto the train. This is when it all began. A man behind him, fiftyish and wearing a flat cap, said in quite a cheeky, and what I instantly thought of as unnecessary, way, "Are you going to let me on then Winkle?" (immediate thought: what on earth does 'Winkle' mean? I later found out it is a child's reference to a penis).

Unfortunately, the other man, who I'll call Winkle (eek), replied with, "Who the f*** is Winkle?". This response was probably a bit defensive, erring on aggressive.

Cheeky chap: You better watch your filthy mouth before I knock you out!

Winkle: Oh really. Go on then; knock me out, right in the face. I'll even give you a free shot, with my arms down. Come on, knock me out!

Cheeky chap: Maybe you should have let me on the train a bit earlier, idiot.

Winkle: Maybe I was being polite and letting other people get off first.

Cheeky chap: Oh that's right, you're the bigger man. You need to learn to respect your elders and not swear.

Winkle: I did. You wanted to knock me out so I said you could. That's being polite, so come on, knock me out.

Cheeky chap: Stop being a c***, you shouldn't have blocked me getting on the train.

Winkle: You better watch what you're saying old man, I told you I was being polite and you started on me by calling me Winkle. If you'd said that to some youths, you would have ended up being knifed you f***ing idiot!

Cheeky chap: Is that right?

Winkle: I'm just saying, you're lucky I'm a polite person *(Do polite people swear this often?)*, some youths would have reacted differently and you'd be in hospital by now.

Cheeky chap: Yeah, well, whatever big man.

SILENCE (11 seconds)

My god the tension in the carriage was similar to that of someone trying to re-string a guitar - twisting it too tight and getting the feeling that at any moment it could snap and poke you in the eye. I was praying - pleading even - that they would keep their mouths shut for the remainder of the journey.

Cheeky chap: Well, I hope you're getting off at the next stop.

Winkle: It's your lucky day, I am!

Cheeky chap: Thank f*** for that.

Yes! This unnecessary row could stop. Like all the other people in the carriage, I could not wait for the awkwardness to end. However, inevitably, it seemed that they both wanted to have the last word:

Winkle: Oh shut up you old f***ing c**t before I knock you out.

Cheeky chap: I could knock your mum up if you want. I'd even throw in some a**l, I'm sure she'd like that.

Winkle: You f***ing twat!

As the train finally arrived at Kentish town, the doors opened and Winkle turned back to shout a final "You f***ing twat," before landing a sturdy-looking punch on Cheeky Chap's shoulder and then cowardly legging it. Cheeky Chap stumbled into a lady and his hat fell off. He turned his face around in response but knew he couldn't do anything as the doors then closed.

I looked around to gauge the reactions of the other witnesses, some in shock, but most still listening to their music, completely oblivious to the masculine bravado that had just unfolded before us.

No-one said *anything*.

The situation had escalated so fast from one inappropriate comment and a lot of unnecessary name calling and swearing, to an assault; all in the space of four minutes. Not one commuter said anything, bearing in mind what they had just witnessed. Everyone stuck to the Commuter Rules, which gave me a momentary feeling of sadness. I think there are maybe some occasions where people should break those rules and realise what has just happened right in front of them and deal with it like compassionate human beings should. No-one even asked how Cheeky Chap was or checked if he was alright, a phenomenon known as 'bystander apathy'.

I'm embarrassed to admit that I have become one of those commuters. My justifications, which were probably like others' in the carriage were:

1) He appeared okay, if not a tad embarrassed.
2) Honestly, they were both idiots and so I didn't feel much sympathy towards either of them.
3) It just made me feel **nothing**. The whole situation was odd and got me wondering how such a little thing could lead to that result. It's a strange world that we live in sometimes.

I still have no idea why this happened, but I know it could have been easily avoided and it left me feeling downbeat about society and myself. Why are people so hostile towards one another, particularly on the tube? Why can't people just be nice? Is it that hard to get along with fellow human beings? Sure, we all have our hard days, when we're stressed or not feeling well, but I wonder how those guys feel now. Do they feel better after that incident? More macho? I hope not, because what I saw happen in such a short space of time was disgusting and disgraceful. It is something that I never want to see again.

\<Casual Racism\>

What are you supposed to do when an individual has decided to be totally disrespectful to somebody else?

This evening started as an average, dull tube journey. I was casually enjoying the last couple of chapters of my book, thinking about what to have for dinner, when an argument appeared to be brewing at the end of the carriage. I leaned over to inspect the individuals involved, as did the rest of the carriage (some may refer to this in the driving world as 'rubber-necking'). Any raised voices will normally lead to this.

It started with a few casual remarks between a man and a woman, the man having just squashed himself on, aggressively shouting "Move Up!" down the packed carriage. He then decided to bundle into the woman next to him, knocking her flashy, expensive looking phone onto the floor. "Idiot" she muttered under her breath. That didn't go down too well. "What did you just say to me woman?". At this point, I was very glad to be sitting a reasonable distance away from them. If the situation exploded then at least my fellow commuters would have to deal with it. Pah! Unlikely.

The situation started to escalate. I didn't catch the woman's response, but let's just say by the facial reaction of the man (creased forehead, unblinking fury in his eyes) that he didn't like it. I think it is important to inform you at this point that he was a white male: scruffy, in his mid-50s with brown/grey unwashed hair, old Reebok trainers and some age-old (presumably, never before taken off) jogging bottoms. The lady was one of the business types: fully suited and booted with killer heels and a designer handbag. She was also black. Here is how the conversation went:

Man: You said f***ing what to me you dirty n*****?
(Loudly)
Woman: Sorry, you called me what?
Man: You heard, why don't you go back to your own country or clean the sh** out of my toilet?
Woman: I was born in this country and so were my family.
Man: Whatever, you've got a nerve taking all our good jobs and ruining this country.
Woman: Coming from you, who looks like such a successful and fantastic person?
Man: Just shut your f***ing mouth you dirty, black sl** before I knock your teeth out!

Meanwhile, the position of every passengers' jaws said it all – hitting the floor. As the man's aggression and insults failed to retreat, shocked faces of "Did he just say that?" and angst spread throughout the carriage.

So, back to my original question, what are you supposed to do in these situations?

One commuter was slyly recording the whole incident on her phone but that wasn't exactly going to help calm the situation down. This appeared to be heading towards violence.

Completely shocked to have played witness to such obvious racism in the present day, I asked myself – how can people still think like this? I could feel my anger levels steadily rising. What could I possibly do to improve the situation? Chances are if I intervened I'd make the whole situation worse and end up in hospital with a black eye and a criminal record. Deep breaths. Breathe in, breathe out. Ignore him.

"Oi, do you mind keeping your racist opinions to yourself please?" spoke the man standing next to him.
"It's not worth it mate," came comments from others around him.
"Calm down everyone," from another bystander.

The tension was building.

The man replied with "You can all shut your f***ing mouths or I'll beat the sh** out of this n*****."

Well, that didn't go down too well.

In stepped a rather built, suited man, who waited until the tube stopped and the doors opened before picking the racist man up, and dumping him on the platform. He then blocked him from getting back on as the doors closed. The lady smiled, the carriage laughed and everyone waved goodbye as the train left the platform.

It was a relief to see that even within the unique environment of the London Underground, there's a level of aggression and abuse that people just won't stand for. My faith in humanity was thankfully restored.

Stop 15: The Art of Getting a Seat

Not only do we have to pay a considerable amount of money to travel to work, but we also have to engage in a form of tai chi to win a much coveted seat.

It's not ideal having to stand up for forty minutes, struggling to keep your balance, especially if you're trying to write a book. You should have seen my first drafts - a mixture of highly-illegible scribbles of a similar standard to those of a three-year-old. I think polar bears would be able to write clearer sentences.

So anyway, let's get back to the main point of this entry before I go off on a tangent and start writing more things I can't read.

Here are some tips on how to nab yourself a seat during a rush hour tube journey.

Firstly, when the train pulls into the station, keep a sharp eye out for any possible gaps, or for a prime standing spot in the pack. If possible, when venturing onto the train, try your best to stand in the middle of the carriage, as this will give you a clear line of sight to at least four potential seats that could come up for grabs.

Right, so say you now have four potential seats. It is *vital* to remain aware of your surroundings at all times. Whenever the train comes close to pulling into a stop, be on the lookout, ready to pounce like a cat on a mouse. However, remember that you're not trying to kill anyone and leave them on the front doorstep. We're just talking about pouncing on the seat here. Also, don't then piss on the seat to mark your territory, that isn't cool (although it may guarantee you a seat, albeit a smelly one).

Normally 'The Seat Mover', a traditional old-age ritual signifying the start of 'The Shuffle' (a transitional period of hope, followed by seat comfort or bum disappointment) begins when the announcement is made over the tannoy "The next stop is 'blah blah'," (don't worry, that isn't an official London Underground stop). Anyone who is due to get off at the next stop will be doing one of the following: shuffling a paper and then placing it behind their head, putting a book in their bag, depositing their phone back into a pocket, or just being generally fidgety. These are the obvious signs. However, like anything in the world of public transport, there are some exceptions to the rule.

Beware of 'The Phantom': an individual, or group of people, who will show you absolutely no signs that they are getting off. The train pulls in, stops, and the person proceeds to fly off, vanishing into thin air like a well-practised magician. There are also those that practise 'The Shuffle' without any intention or need to leave the carriage. A very sly and confusing bunch, 'The No Directioners' tease us 'Standees' by hovering over their seats, collecting their valuables and completely upsetting our seat radars.

Alert! Alert!
Potential seat available!

All 'Standees' eyes are glued to 'The No Directioner', twitching with the anticipation of a warm, worn and overused cushion for their tired and frustrated limbs. Only for them to then sit back down and offer no explanation for their irrational movements. At this point, you will need to control that little bit of rage that has manifested itself in your head. Otherwise, you may miss the opportunity to spot 'The Seat Mover' behind you who is getting up and leaving.

Most importantly, remember to remain calm, stay alert and be nippy. Just like in tai chi, know your surroundings. Today I tested my theory and it worked.

SUCCESS!!

The seat was a bit damp and smelly, but definitely worth it.

Stop 16: Happy Birthday Tubey!

Happy birthday to the tube, happy birthday to the tube, happy birthday dearest tubey, happy birthday to you (cue loud clapping, party poppers, balloons and a train-themed cake)!

On 9 January 2013, the tube turned 150 years old (not looking too shabby for its age).

It's come a long way since the first train in 1863 on the Metropolitan Railway. I loved one article I read that managed to locate a letter of complaint from a passenger after the first week of it being open, quoting exactly the same problems that we face today: overcrowding, delays, having to wait too long between trains and sweaty, smelly armpits. Who'd have thought we'd have the same complaints over 150 years later?

It is hardly ever recognised how amazing the London Underground really is, carrying the same number of passengers annually as the whole rest of the country's rail network combined. Who'd have thought we'd have over 1.37 billion people using it every year?

To highlight how fantastic old tubey is, here are some fascinating stats[2]:

Length of network	402 kilometres
Busiest station	Waterloo - 100.3 million passengers per year
Annual train kilometres travelled	83.6 million kilometres
Average train speed	33kph
Proportion of network in tunnels	45%
Longest continuous tunnel	East Finchley to Morden (via Bank) - 27.8 kilometres
Total number of passenger escalators	440
Station with most escalators	Waterloo - 23
Longest escalator	Angel - 60 metres
Shortest escalator	Stratford - 4.1 metres
Total number of passenger lifts	188
Step-free stations	72
Station with most platforms	Baker Street – 10
Highest station above mean sea level	Amersham (Metropolitan line) - 147 metres

---

[2] Facts and figures obtained from https://tfl.gov.uk/corporate/about-tfl/what-we-do/london-underground/facts-and-figures

Furthest station from central London	Chesham (Metropolitan line) – 47 kilometres to Aldgate
Longest distance between stations	Chesham to Chalfont & Latimer (Metropolitan line) - 6.3 kilometres
Shortest distance between stations	Leicester Square to Covent Garden (Piccadilly line) - 0.3 kilometres
Longest direct journey	Epping to West Ruislip (Central line) - 54.9 kilometres

How about a few alternative facts[3] to liven up the party?

1) The American talk show host Jerry Springer was born at East Finchley station during the Second World War – aiming for peace from an early age.
2) Half a million mice are estimated to live in the Underground system – leave the cheese at home.
3) According to TFL, London Underground trains travel a total of 1,735 times around the world (or 90 trips to the moon and back) each year – beat that NASA.
4) In cockney rhyming slang, the London Underground is known as the Oxo (Cube/Tube) – take stock - surely there's some advertising potential here?

---

[3] Alternative facts and figures obtained from https://www.telegraph.co.uk/travel/destinations/europe/united-kingdom/england/london/articles/London-Underground-150-fascinating-Tube-facts/

Pretty impressive facts and figures right? So, as you travel on your journey into work today, appreciate the success of this network and not complain about it.

Well, for one day at least. Who wants a goody bag?

Stop 17: Germtastic

Germs. Ever thought about the number of germs flying around in this underground world? Nope, neither have I. Well, until today that is. Warning! Probably best not to read this segment while eating your brekkie.

Going through my normal daily routine, I boarded my tube train and someone immediately coughed in my face. Lovely. The cough was gunky and flemy sounding and even included a little bit of visible vapour, like an extra topping that you'd get on an ice cream sundae. I subsequently rubbed my face down with my coat and then placed a clean hand onto a rail to help my balance. Big mistake. The moment my fingertips came into contact with the rail I knew something was up as my hand felt sticky and moist. I consider myself to have quite speedy reactions, so it was touch on, touch off within a second. Peering over at where my hand had just been, I saw a deep red stain. Oh fantastic. I wasn't willing to investigate any further, as unfortunately I had forgotten my CSI kit and couldn't take any samples. However, my instinct told me it was one of two things: either ketchup from an evening burger/morning treat or... I'd rather not think about it. I prayed it was the former but wasn't planning on licking my fingers to find out.

So, for the second time today, I rubbed myself down, but this time with a spare tissue I found in my pocket. Only at this point did I contemplate just how dirty the tube may be. Imagine how many people hold onto that rail every day, sit on that seat, or sneeze and cough in those carriages. How often does each train get cleaned?

Best not to think about it so let's move on el rapido.

On a related note, do you ever find that when it's really busy the handrails always appear to be in an awkward place above your head or next to someone's face or crotch? This often leads to a clear view of sweaty armpits (yuck) or uncomfortable moments as you try to find a section of the handrail that isn't located within the vicinity of a fellow passenger's private area. What about people of the tiny variety? If they're stuck in the middle and there isn't a side rail to hold onto, then they're at an increased risk of being thrown into all kinds of hilarious moving/stumbling/falling over incidents, or even moshing as if they were in a crowded festival listening to Metallica.

What's more, whenever you find a spot on the handrail then take your hand off for a split second (to turn your page, re-adjust your coat or try to get the blood supply back into your hand) and then go to put it back – Boom! – your hand lands rather awkwardly on somebody else's. You look over, hoping it'll be someone stunningly beautiful, giving you a beaming smile and a cheeky wink. Nah. It's just a dirty old man in a mac holding a torn plastic bag. So, there you are, trying to avoid eye contact, desperately attempting to find another spot on the handrail before you fall over and embarrass yourself.

Anyhow, back on topic - just to top off the day of germs, when on the travellator, I noticed I was being followed by the most menacing of things.

It was long, white and had a tail.

It was... a *tampon.*

That's right everyone, someone had left a *tampon* on the travellator. Delightful. Something that I wasn't expecting to see first thing in the morning. The way it moved did remind me of playing poo sticks when I was a young-un'. This thought, for a split second, made me consider picking the tampon up and putting it back on the opposite travellator to see the reactions it would get from my fellow commuters. However, I then remembered the stain on the handrail I had encountered earlier, and that seemingly genius idea swiftly vanished from my mind.

Tube Announcement:

"We'll be held at this page for an indefinite period of time, for absolutely no reason. Enjoy the view."

\<Mind the Gap\>

Stop 18: European Differences: Berlin

Guten tag Deutschland. Mein hamster ist gestorben und wo kann ich bier? Those are the only two phrases that I knew before I visited Berlin. I always like to make an effort to learn a bit of the language before I visit a foreign country, so I thought these two phrases would put me in good stead to make a few friends.

Time to compare the London Underground with a European counterpart.

Just to put this into context: this venture was a stag do so there was no plan to make our two-day visit cultural. The only word that was important was bier and bier only.

We were all designated jobs for the weekend. The stag was obviously 'shot-man', my friend was 'chief pap', another was 'IT Support' (that is, he had the only phone and his duty was to help us if we were lost or needed to find somewhere) and I was, as the only 'Londoner' of the group, 'Uber-bahn boy'. The Uber-bahn is Berlin's equivalent of the tube. It's actually called the U-bahn, but one of the guys started naming it that and no matter how many times we told him, "Stop being an idiot, it's the U-bahn," he just didn't get it.

So, reluctantly, as the 'Uber-bahn boy', I grabbed a map and was pleasantly surprised to see that the general outlook of the Berlin Underground system was relatively similar to the tubes of London. For example, one of the lines going through the centre was red... two lines go around the city in a circular format... one goes direct from south to north and splits into two... You get the point. Let's just say I felt in my element and completely up to the task at hand.

After a few minutes of being on the U-bahn, we did immediately notice something different, which frequented each train journey during that weekend. Bands would appear, turn on a CD, play an instrument and start singing. My personal favourite was a rendition of "Superstitious" by Stevie Wonder. They somehow managed to incorporate a rap into it.

Unfortunately, they would only play in the carriage for one stop, ask for money and then move onto the next, so you never got to listen to a whole song. On average, three people paid them per carriage. We tried to calculate whether this amounted to them making a reasonable living if they did this every day, jumping carriages, for ten hours. We thought it'd be enough to get a stein of beer and a few bratwurst, so definitely worth it.

Music seemed to be a common theme in el Germania. Even on the normal overground trains, every time you were about to pull up to a stop, the tannoy would play some little jingle before they informed the passengers as to which stop they were approaching. Very jolly. Perhaps London should think about incorporating this into our tube service? In the morning, we could start with some easy listening music (Bob Marley) to warm everyone up, but then move onto heavier beats to get you pumped (or when your coffee kicks in). Lunchtime travellers could experience tourist music; basically just play the national anthem, Adele or Ed Sheeran. The evening commuter could then wind down with some classical music, to keep everybody calm and un-confrontational.

Another key difference I noticed between Berlin and London is the ticketing system. They have not (yet) employed the Oyster or contactless payment system. Instead, you buy a ticket from a machine and then stamp it yourself at stations. On the first day we felt it was pointless buying a ticket as we used the U-bahn about 8-9 times and saw no inspectors. After we had gone back to the hotel to freshen up (including sinking a few more beers), we returned to the station and contemplated not purchasing a ticket. Thank god the sensible one out of us all made us buy one (me!). Within a minute of alighting, adorning a pair of plain denim jeans and an equally in-descript polo shirt, a chap came storming through the carriage. Were it not for the ticket machine bouncing off his hip like an uncontrollable toddler, I would not have known that he was an inspector. He was a skin-head, with tattoos all over his arms, and generally looked like a guy that you don't mess with.

We showed him our valid tickets and he moved on to an American guy (early twenties). However, it quickly became apparent he did not have a ticket. What they say about strict Germans is true. When the frightened American asked if he could buy a ticket there and then, the response was extremely stern. "It is illegal to not buy a ticket before you travel on German trains, you will get off at the next stop and we will call the police."

Ahhhh!!!

We all looked at each other with a huge sense of relief spread across our faces. This man was terrifying! The next stop came, they both got off and the police were already on the platform waiting. I couldn't help but think what a great stag story that could have been: getting arrested for failing to pay a train ticket...

It seems that the Berlin commuter population have never seen Morph suits. The final night of our beer-infested weekend entailed donning these all-in-one body suits to hit the streets. We'd never had so many people come and ask to have their pictures taken with us – we were like celebrities (D-list at best). To be fair, most people thought we were the Power Rangers and demanded a performance. We decided to give the crowd what they were obviously oh so desperate for and proceeded to perform highly humiliating poses and dances (as an ensemble of course). They all seemed to find it entertaining. We were tempted to ask for some donations for the night (we fancied some free steins and bratwursts), but I don't think our entertainment was equal to that of the musical bands on the trains seen earlier that day.

I did learn one extra phrase from the friendly Berlin people – "Du riechst wie ein esel" – which they told me translates to – "You're a great dancer" (I'd like to believe that was true…).

Overall, we had a great time on the German equivalent of the London Underground.

Danke und auf wiedersehen.

\<Change lines\>

Stop 19: Indecent Exposure

\<Carrot and Bean Casserole\>

Halfway through a journey we came to a sudden halt. The driver announced that there was a fault with the train and that we must wait for any updates. Super. An indefinite amount of time then; it could be anything from thirty seconds to two hours.

After two minutes, a fellow commuter (I'll refer to him as Mr Truffle) decided to stand up and announce to the entire carriage that he needed to go for "A number two," and "There is no way I can hold it in for any longer." I can't even attempt to put into words my reaction to that. All I kept thinking was – how desperate must he have been to stand up and announce it to everyone? Making such a drastic decision was surely based on the prospect of having no quick escape route to a toilet.

Take a moment and ask yourself - what would you do in his shoes? Would you do the same or quietly eek one out and let the people around you make assumptions based on the smell? Either way, it's a pretty dire and messy situation to be in.

People began to edge away from Mr Truffle – well, as best they could on a heavily crowded commuter train - feeling nervous about what the immediate future would bring. Others, to my surprise, began troubleshooting, and started to direct him towards one of the windows of the carriage. My brain was working on overdrive, trying to figure out what they were attempting to achieve – open the window and throw him out?

What transpired next was a very logical way of dealing with a unique situation. The window was cranked opened for ventilation purposes. Four people then gathered up some copies of the Evening Standard and created a barrier around Mr Truffle, shielding his bottom half from view. Some of the pages were also put on the floor underneath him.

He proceeded to pull his trousers down, squatted, and did his business onto the back cover of the Evening Standard. Ironically, it was a story about how terrible Arsenal had played the night before.

'The business' was swiftly scooped up and thrown out of the window (not into the opposite carriage, thankfully). Trousers went back up. Mr Truffle looked especially relieved.

Then, as if by magic, the super poo fuelled the engine and within seconds of it splattering across the tracks, the train exploded back into action and we were on the move again. I would have been thankful for the extra home-propelling gas if it were not for the warm and lingering smoky stench of egg and carrots that accompanied it.

Needless to say, I didn't have casserole for dinner.

\<Girls, Girls, Girls\>

So, we were getting the tube to Camden at 7:30pm the other night. Note I said 7:30pm, so not that late. I casually plonked my bum on a superb quality Northern line train seat next to my partner in crime (we don't undertake in criminal activities, I just mean she is my girlfriend). When we arrived at Archway my fellow companion gave me a nudge and whispered (well, spoke at a normal level as the noise of the tube was so loud).

"When you get a chance, slyly look to your right at the next carriage."

My initial thought was – look to the right, look to the right! However, I managed to control myself and wait a few seconds before I cautiously and casually, manoeuvered my head to the right.

Criiii-keeey-O-Riley. I wasn't expecting that.

Can you believe it? No, neither could I.

A middle-aged, slightly over-weight woman, thought it'd be fun to squash her boobs up against the windows in-between the carriages. I know the tube can sometimes get hot, but come on...

When she wandered away from the window, they fell back into place, resting on her belly. She was having a great time, stumbling all over the carriage and falling into who I can only (hopefully) assume were here friends. Drunk at this hour? It is only 7:30pm, she must have started early!

At this point my girlfriend suggested that we should, to be on the safe side, look away in case we caught her eye and she decided to grace us with her full-frontal presence. I obeyed, as I didn't fancy some sweaty boobs planted on my face.

Unsurprisingly, she crossed carriages but made a right pig's ear of it. After some agonising moments, she managed to gain enough balance to cross the divide and ungracefully step into our carriage. She then proceeded to stumble and fall onto a fairly handsome looking chap. The wind appeared to have been completely knocked out of him.

"Alright love, you're gorgeous, do you wanna see my boobs?"

Before he had any chance to respond...

Boom!

Out they were, right in his face.

This was followed by laughter and a random announcement of - "I've got two kids you know, two kids" (cue more laughter).

Errrrrm...

What kind of response did she expect from that statement - a high five or boob ten? I imagined what her children would say if they could see her there in all her glory - "Mum. Mum! What are you doing? Muuuuum!!!"

To be fair to the man she was conversing with, he handled the situation well and politely chatted to her, frequently adding "Your friends are asking for you," after every sentence. She finally got the hint and stumbled back to her friends.

My final, lasting memory of this journey was the same woman lifting her top up and then accidentally barging into a poor, innocent and completely unaware old lady getting onto the tube. I bet she won't be forgetting that titillating sight any time soon.

\<Public Displays of Affection\>

Late one evening on my way home, I observed a fascinating couple sat opposite me, who had decided to initiate their mating rituals with some passionate smooching in a very public place (my carriage). Not only that, but they must have been in their mid-forties and were a peculiar couple to place together.

I'm not the world's greatest descriptive author, so I thought I'd draw you some illustrations:

As you can tell by my fantastic sketches, the man was tall, thin and had a very square head. Whereas the lady was small, cuddly, and well, just round. Did I mention that they both looked clammy? (I didn't want to ask why.)

So, now imagine how mesmerising it was to watch their love and passion for each other unfold in front of the normal, everyday commuter's eye. It was like watching two teenagers at it for the first time and, incredibly, there was even a cheeky grope! It's amazing what lust can do to you; apparently for Kylie and Jason over there, it has the power to remove any typically British (or just normal) embarrassment they may have felt participating in displays of such affection in a public place. They were all over each other, non-stop touching, kissing and snuggling.

Awkward. I felt like I was intruding on some secret, romantic weekend away.

My aim was to get off the train as quickly as possible. It was not pleasant viewing. People need to learn to get a room - a private room that is, not a tube carriage. Fingers crossed they get married and move to a nice place in the country as soon as possible. I don't want to witness that sort of hanky-panky on my way to work every day.

Stop 20: Creature Comforts

\<Animal Travellers\>

Some days can be bizarre. Today was one of those days. The bus was delayed so I was left with no choice but to take a nice 15-minute stroll down a petrol-fumed street, where I was cut up by no less than three black cats. Three. Black. Cats. See how they run? They weren't running. Bad omen? I know what you're thinking - same cat. Very unlikely, but if so, it must have been very nimble and had a vendetta against me.

From there I couldn't really prepare myself for what I saw next. It was perched on a woman's shoulder. Parrot you ask? Feathered bird? Incorrect! It was a spider monkey. You heard me, a *spider monkey*. Can you believe that? On the tube? A woman was getting on at rush hour with a monkey on her shoulder! Thankfully, it was well behaved. A good, if a little bit of a cheeky commuter, it remained silent throughout the journey. It did have its eye on a lady eating a banana and a young man drinking an Um Bongo. Impressively, it managed to control itself.

Later, on the way home, a couple stumbled onto the train, wearing torn, disheveled clothes and holding cans of nondescript lager. The aura that encapsulated them and surrounded the nearby atmosphere was intoxicating. Hence, I was forced to cough a couple of times and discreetly hold my nose.

They were accompanied by a furry friend: a short, brown-haired canine with a spiked collar. The couple sat down and called the dog up to take the last remaining seat (bear in mind this was the last available seat on a rush hour tube journey). Quite a few dirty looks appeared on the faces of commuters.

A young lady boarded the train at the next stop and politely asked if she could sit down.

"Nope, dog is sitting there."

At this point the dog leapt off the seat. The couple immediately tried calling it back, but it wasn't interested in the slightest. Or it was - unlike its owners - being polite. The lady took the opportunity to try and take the empty seat but was then faced with an overly aggressive response. The couple barked that they had bought a ticket and so their dog was entitled to the seat. Huh? I'm not sure how they came to that conclusion – had they bought an extra ticket just for the dog? In the end the lady gave up, obviously not wanting to get involved with any further confrontation over something so silly as a dog getting priority seating.

While watching this unfold in front of me, all these images of dogs sitting on the tube suddenly popped into my head. Just like in the series of paintings entitled 'Dogs Playing Poker', by Cassius Marcellus Coolidge. I imagined them craftily adapted to fit the tube, such as dogs wearing suits and holding briefcases, listening to music, reading the paper etc - you get the picture.

So, you'd think that would be enough for one day right? **NAH**! There was one final, remaining animal treat for me on the way home (Whimzees anyone?). As the doors opened at East Finchley and I stepped off onto a rather windy platform, a mouse sprinted onto the train. I walked away smiling to myself and heard a chorus of high-pitched screams, quickly followed by the 'beep beep' of the doors closing.

Eeeeek.

\<Hakuna Matata\>

Have you ever thought that when a train empties, it's a bit like a stampede? You know, like that one in the Lion King? You remember when Mufasa gets killed? How can we forget that? I'm getting emotional just thinking about it...

Today really reminded me of that scene. I was trying to walk against a sudden influx of London commuters who were all moving very quickly as one unit. It looked impressive and intimidating at the same time.

A little advice: always keep a tight hold of your bag, as it could at any minute - like Mufasa (weep) - be swept away by the stampede and you will never see it again (apart from maybe on a lovely starry night).

Also, never forget that in London you unfortunately won't have the comforting accompaniment of Timon and Pumba singing 'Hakuna Matata' to cheer you up when you've lost your bag (unless, that is, you have the soundtrack close to hand).

Stop 21: The Bus

\<Angry Drivers\>

It was Shrove Tuesday, and I casually strolled to my bus stop (just to confirm, I don't own it) and from a distance noticed that it was busier than usual. I looked up at the board that showed the times and apparently five buses were 'due'.

Ten minutes later, a bus finally arrived and everyone bundled on in the usual fashion. I decided to wait for the next 'due' bus as using my commuter instinct, it should overtake the current bus and arrive at my destination (Archway station) first.

When I embarked, I couldn't help but notice that the bus driver seemed a dash aggrieved. His face was a picture: harsh, shrewd eyes and a mouth that was quite the upside-down smile. One person dared not have an Oyster card and wanted to pay in cash. Crikey, what a disaster (this was back in the days when you could still pay in cash. Mental I know). I could hear the driver groaning as the cogs in his brain frantically attempted to calculate the correct change, which he then proceeded to slam down in the slot with passionate force.

Almost immediately after the bus pulled away from the stop, the bell rang, then rang again... and again (you can see where this is going). It may be best to describe this in the form of a little song for you, to a tune you may recognise:

"The bell on the bus goes ding, ding, ding,
ding, ding, ding,
ding, ding ding.
The bell on the bus goes ding, ding, ding...
and the bus driver says f*** under his breath."

The driver's sheer frustration and anger was quite the sight to see. He was glowing purple like a beetroot, with deep creases across his forehead that made his eyes disappear into his face.

At the next stop, a lady had been waiting at the back doors, ready to push her pram on. After politely waiting for her fellow passengers to pass, the driver subsequently closed the doors. So, she then knocked on the window and asked the driver to open the doors again. I swear to god his facial reaction was akin to someone telling him that his wife had been attacked by a giant lemon and so there were to be no pancakes for dinner. He looked *that* annoyed.

His final response was a frustrated nod as he pressed the button to release the tired doors.

Obviously he couldn't muster up any speech due to shock and the fact that he'd had to use his brain once already that morning.

Flippin' hell.

<Teenage maturity... not!>

On the way home yesterday, some skinny, baggy-jean-wearing youths (I know, I'm starting to sound like my dad...) attempted a scheme to get on the bus without paying. Basically, one tried to use a fake Oyster card while two others claimed to have valid tickets and they didn't need to show them. They all ran upstairs.

No movement from the bus.

The driver was having none of it. Basically, we weren't moving until they paid or disembarked. Not really what you need when you've been up since 5am, working like a maniac; I just wanted to launch onto the sofa and watch some trash TV (Celeb's Go Dating anyone?).

1 minute.

Another call out.

2 minutes.

No movement.

3 minutes.

Another call out.

People start getting off the bus.

4 minutes.

"Oh, for god's sake, how much do I need to pay for you to move?" said an irritated lady as she started to get her purse out. Nope, the bus driver wasn't allowing that and continued on stubbornly.

5 minutes.
Another call out.

Finally, some movement. Cue loud stomps from above and down the stairs.

The teenagers ran out of the front door at full pace, hitting the glass front that protects the driver with some force, so much so that it was left wobbling and making a noise like someone playing the didgeridoo.

So mature (I think I have now successfully become my dad).

<Old School Aggression>

People on buses can be such idiots sometimes.

Mr Khan, please can you make an 'Ignorabus' so they can all get on together, rather than ruin our British polite, quiet journeys?

This morning's ruined journey was based around two people.

The first was a middle-aged, slightly overweight lady with greasy hair and a stinking, miserable look on her face.

The second was an old man (in his eighties), quite tall and slim, with broad shoulders and a huge overcoat. He slowly stepped onto the bus thanks to the aid of a shabby looking walking stick. The lady was sitting by the window, and so the elderly chap (let's call him Bob-dy-bob) sat next to her (let's call her Dully). It all began peacefully.

Cue a couple of sideways glances by Dully followed by a little nudge to the shoulder, and then a **full-on scream** at the top of her lungs:

"What is wrong with you?!? Stop f***ing touching and nudging me you dirty old man."

Not much of a response from Bob-dy-bob.

"Stop it, you sad old man, just go home. Go home."

A confused, and rather shocked look spread over Bob-dy-Bob's face.

At this point, passengers around me began to twitch.

SILENCE

Two minutes passed and everything returned to a state of relative calmness but there remained a strong sense of awkwardness in the air. Everyone was thinking the same thing – this wouldn't end here. We all prayed that one of them quickly departed before it all kicked off again.

Unsurprisingly, it did all kick off again. Yay.

Dully nudged Bob-dy-bob, and exuded a high-pitched scream (cue ear drums bursting). Then, in one final desperate attempt to rid herself of Bob, she gave him the almightiest shove, to which he lost his balance and crumpled onto the floor of the gangway adjacent to the stairs. This immediately sparked an aggrieved response from the lady in front, who strongly informed Dully how you shouldn't do that to a frail, old man. She was having none of it, standing up, pointing at Bob-dy-bob and continuing to shout and swear.

Down the stairs came a ten-year-old boy. He quickly rushed to the old man's aid and tried his best to help lift him up. Unfortunately, he just couldn't manage it alone (obviously he'd skipped the gym for the last two months preferring to play Lego and eat cheese, and so the 'Swans' weren't in good enough shape). In the background, Dully was still F-ing and blinding relentlessly.

Enter the boy's dad, whose first image of the scene was his son trying his almighty best to help lift an old man off the floor, whilst a lady was standing over him screaming.

One look by the dad. That is all it took.

Suddenly there was silence from Dully. The dad informed the driver to report an assault and to call the police.

One look. All over.

\<You Say Pub, I Say Quiz\>

You know when you go to a pub quiz regularly and it's basically impossible to win? There's always one team, The Regulars, who are there week in, week out and unless they're absent (mysteriously contracted food poisoning or something...), you've got no chance in hell of taking home the prized jackpot (three cans of an energy drink and a £10 M&S voucher).

Within the group of 'The Regulars', there is normally one guy who just 'happens' to know everything: from who was number one in the charts on Christmas day 1982, to who scored the first goal when Liverpool made their comeback against AC Milan in the 2005 Champions League Final. He knows *everything*.

He gets my bus.

Yes, that's right, I think I witnessed one of these creatures swatting up on a bit of research, out of their natural habitat (surrounded by flat, expensive beer and rowdy friends winding down after work), on the 43 bus to London Bridge. I am not kidding when I say he was reading a book entitled 'Pub Quiz: round 2', which (having a peak over his shoulder) *only* contained questions and answers. That was all he was reading, questions and answers!

Anyway, here are a few of the questions that I noticed in his book:

1) What is the pirate's flag with the skull and cross-bones called?
2) Which port provided a hit for The Beautiful South?
3) What is the translation of 'Mein Kampf', the book which set out Hitler's political creed?
4) Who wrote 'The War of the Worlds'?
5) What is the best cartoon programme ever?[4]

If you got those right without cheating (which includes using smartphones), then get yourself down to a pub quiz near you, NOW!

Just think how energised you would feel and how many new bras you could get with those M&S vouchers (... not even one!).

---

[4] Answers: 1) Jolly Roger, 2) Rotterdam, 3) My Struggle, 4) H.G. Wells and 5) Not strictly a proper question and not based on anything but my opinion – Wacky Races, Thundercats, Family Guy?

<(minor) Celeb Spot>

I saw Les Dennis on the 134 bus today. That's right, Les Dennis. Les Deeeeeeeeeennis. Family Fortunes was his forte, and what a show that was!

I was extremely tempted to push my way through to him and say, "We've asked 100 people to name who they would most like to sit next to on the 134 bus to work." I didn't have the nerve - I respected his privacy. He'd better appreciate that. Instead, I tried to think of my top five answers to that survey question (in no particular order):

1) Donald Trump – for all those times that you get really annoyed while commuting and you feel like punching someone in the face.
2) Usain Bolt – fastest man ever. But then, at the speed he can travel, running would prove quicker than travelling on a London bus.
3) Rachel Stevens – no reason whatsoever. NO REASON.
4) Michel Roux – supplying Michelin starred food for my commute into work. Top travel breakfast.
5) Stevie Wonder – the Master Blaster himself. To provide awesome music to liven up an otherwise dull journey and to get everyone up showing off their best dance moves.

Who would you pick? I hope none of you even considered the likes of Justin Bieber, the Teletubbies or 'for a laugh', Les Dennis.

\<The Night Bus\>

Everyone has a cracking story from a London night bus, right? Here are my top picks.

Bus Boy Racer

It was a Saturday night. ***Correction*** Sunday morning. 4am to be precise. My girlfriend and I had finished our evening in Hoxton and waited for our bus back from Old Street. It arrived and we got on with no qualms. The driver just seemed like your average moody guy considering the time of the morning.

The fun began when the bus started moving.

The bus was being driven, ***Correction***, drag-raced, down the roads at high speeds. It was like participating in an episode of Top Gear, where there's a race-off between a London bus and a drunken skateboarder.

I felt for those poor buggers standing up who were bearing the brunt of it - especially as they were already slightly, ***Correction***, exceptionally, inebriated. It was bedlam. People were falling over, kebab dinners were flying through the air and stomachs were churning.

To be blunt, the bus driver was being a dick.

To showcase this even further, he decided to skip past two stops for absolutely no reason. This was much to the annoyance of the people who had rightfully pressed the buzzer and were patiently waiting to recover from the breakneck speeds. To say they weren't the least bit impressed, even in their drunken states, was a mild understatement. Cue a lot of shouting, followed by harsh braking. They bundled off, nowhere near a bus stop, swearing their way through the doors.

Thanks to the driver's shenanigans, my girlfriend and I actually managed to arrive home earlier than normal.

Shame we were covered in kebab and lukewarm beer.

The Graveyard Shift

I feel sympathetic for night-bus drivers. It must be like being the sober parent driving his drunk teenager and their friends back home, with the constant worry that someone is going to throw up on your shiny new leather upholstery.

The Graveyard Shift cannot be fun – especially when your route goes through the very popular nightspots. With the sheer number of drunk, drugged up, aggressive people that are likely to step onto the bus and cause trouble, it must be intimidating. All you want to do is sit in your cubicle, drive your route and go home - where you can eat pizza, have a drink, watch a film and hit the hay.

Whereas reality gives you:

1) The Abusers - whether it be because of booze, drugs or having to endure dreadful cheesy music all night, they like to vent their anger by shouting at you.
2) The Vommers - pretty easy to explain - people vomming over your once spotless bus.

3) The Freeloaders - those that skip onto the bus without paying.
4) The Immatureathons - those that press the button a thousand times to the tune of Vindaloo.
5) The Kebabies - where the smell of dead rat meat must make you feel nauseous.
6) The Paraletics - falling onto/over/across the bus and up/down the stairs, possibly leading to "This bus is terminating here," and a trip to the nearest hospital.
7) The Nappers – who fall asleep and don't realise that they've missed their stop until they're at the end of the line. This leaves you feeling responsible and trying to work out a way to make sure they get home safely.
8) The Big Entertainers - who think that singing 'Don't look back in anger' at the top of their lungs at 4:28 in the morning is a great idea (sometimes it is. Definitely Maybe).
9) A combination of all of the above.

Yeah, come to think of it, it must be a pretty tough job. Bring a bucket and two pints of water.

Connection

My girlfriend and I were on a bus heading back to a friend's place for the night, when this guy sitting behind us decided that 2:20am on a Sunday morning was the appropriate time to serenade us with his own versions of the big hits by Take That and the Backstreet Boys. He was passionate. Reeeeeal passionate. It was totally hilarious.

Here are some highlights:

"Everything changes but you" – aimed directly at us.

"I want to go home... that a way. Tell me why?!?" – looking outside.

"Relight my fire!!!" – pointing at a guy outside the window trying to light a cigarette.

I thought that this would be enough randomness for one night, but obviously not. When we stepped off the bus, there were two teenage boys hanging out by a corner shop, looking all shady.

As we cautiously walked past them, hand in hand (aww, so cute), one of the boys (slick back blonde hair and baggy jeans), came out with a fantastic one-liner:

"Have you got Wi-Fi?" (cue confused looks from us)

"Cause I'm not feeling the connection."

Hysterical. Totally unexpected. It certainly got us laughing. If only all journeys ended *that a way*.

Final Stop

That's it guys, the end of the line. It's all over between us. Get over it. Move on. Read a better book. I've reached my final destination and need to go to work now. No more time for documenting all the weird and wonderful happenings while commuting.

When you head home tonight, or manage to drag yourself out of bed tomorrow and attempt the slog to work on the tube or bus, I ask of you two things:

1) Be more aware of your surroundings (you may, like me, witness and experience some entertaining events).
2) Be nicer to your fellow commuter.

This doesn't mean you need to talk to them, just smile every now and again. Offer someone a seat ahead of you if they look like they need it, a tissue if they are upset, or some much needed aqua mineral if they are hungover. Show people that you are still human, even on public transport.

Word of warning to you all, I'm an observant character, and my train of thought does tend to wander slightly. So, the next time something hilarious happens to you on the tube or bus - watch out - as I may be somewhere on your carriage, writing it down!

This book terminates here. Toodles!

About

(If you really care)

The Author

Hi! Thanks to those of you that made it to the end. What a herculean effort. My name is Stephen Down, and I started commuting on the London Underground back in 2010.

As you may have guessed, I'm not much of a writer but the sheer amount of entertainment I noticed from travelling around London inspired me to put it down on paper for you all to enjoy.

If you'd like to keep up-to-date with more bizarre and delightful things I notice on the London Underground, feel free to follow me on Instagram - Downontheunderground.

The Illustrations

All the incredible illustrations that you see throughout this book (apart from the dreadful stick men) were put together by a very talented friend of mine, Paul Jode.

Check him out at http://pauljode.com/ or follow him on Instagram – pauljodedesign.

\<This Book Terminates Here\>

(Adios amigos!)